"I can't stay, Cash. I've put you and everybody else around here in danger."

He tapped the badge that was lying on the counter. "I'm a cop. I'm trained to deal with danger."

"This isn't your situation to deal with," she reminded him. "If I'd been thinking straight, I never would have come here."

He made a rough sound of displeasure and crammed his hands into the pockets of his jeans, making them more snug than they already were. Something Delaney wished she hadn't noticed.

"I won't let you go," he insisted. There wasn't a shred of compromise in his tone.

Her chin automatically came up. "I don't think you have a choice."

Because she didn't want to look at his narrowed amber-brown eyes, Delaney got up and walked to the window. Outside, there were a few ranch hands milling around the barns.

For the moment, she was safe.

MAVERICK JUSTICE

USA TODAY Bestselling Author

DELORES FOSSEN

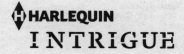

HARLEQUIN

INTRIGUE

HARLEQUIN®
INTRIGUE™

PLEASE RECYCLE
THIS PRODUCT IS RECYCLABLE

Recycling programs
for this product may
not exist in your area.

ISBN-13: 978-1-335-58204-1

Maverick Justice

Copyright © 2022 by Delores Fossen

For questions and comments about the quality of this book, please contact us at CustomerService@Harlequin.com.

Harlequin Enterprises ULC
22 Adelaide St. West, 41st Floor
Toronto, Ontario M5H 4E3, Canada
www.Harlequin.com

Printed in U.S.A.

Delores Fossen, a *USA TODAY* bestselling author, has written over one hundred novels, with millions of copies of her books in print worldwide. She's received a Booksellers' Best Award and an RT Reviewers' Choice Best Book Award. She was also a finalist for a prestigious RITA® Award. You can contact the author through her website at www.deloresfossen.com.

Books by Delores Fossen

Harlequin Intrigue

The Law in Lubbock County

Sheriff in the Saddle
Maverick Justice

Mercy Ridge Lawmen

Her Child to Protect
Safeguarding the Surrogate
Targeting the Deputy
Pursued by the Sheriff

Longview Ridge Ranch

Safety Breach
A Threat to His Family
Settling an Old Score
His Brand of Justice

HQN

Last Ride, Texas

Spring at Saddle Run
Christmas at Colts Creek

Visit the Author Profile page at Harlequin.com.

CAST OF CHARACTERS

Sheriff Cash Mercer—When this Texas lawman reunites with his ex-fiancée after someone tries to murder her, they both become targets of a killer.

Delaney Archer—As a trial lawyer, she lost a case that sent a man to jail. Now that man has escaped, and he could be the one who wants Cash and her dead.

Gil Archer—Delaney's father, who's made no secret that he despises Cash and his family. He might go to any lengths to keep Cash and Delaney apart.

Webb Bennison—He blames Delaney for his conviction of manslaughter, but just how far would he go to get revenge?

Ramone Bennison—Webb's brother, who claims he's not involved in any plan Webb might have for revenge, but he's staying awfully close to Cash and Delaney.

Kevin Byers—This PI has a serious grudge against Delaney for firing him, and he could be behind the attacks to kill Cash and her.

Chapter One

The car was following her.

Delaney Archer was sure of it. She was sure, too, that the black SUV was quickly eating up the distance between them. When it caught up with her, the person inside would try to kill her.

Her too-fast heartbeat throbbed in her ears, and she shook her head, trying to will away the dizziness. She had to stay focused. Alert. Because her life depended on it. If she ran off the road, the killer would have her.

Lightning rifled through the black sky and lit up the sign that told her she was still five miles from the town of Clay Ridge. Too far. And on the rural road, there was nowhere to turn around and try to get back to her house in Lubbock. Besides, it wouldn't be safe there, either. The SUV would just follow her, and since she'd be alone at her home, she would be an easy target.

The thunder came several seconds after the lightning. A thick rumbling groan that sounded like a primal warning. One that she tried hard not to allow to fuel the panic that was racing through her. Just a couple more minutes and then she could see her fiancé, Cash Mercer.

Cash would make all of this better. He always did, and more than ever she needed him. He'd know what to do about the person following her. Cash could stop it because he was the sheriff of Clay Ridge.

She took the road toward Cash's ranch and checked her rearview mirror again. Even with the rain and her spotty vision, Delaney could see the SUV make the turn right behind her. He stayed close. Too close.

Delaney added more pressure to the accelerator and sped through the deep puddles that had already collected on the road. The wipers slashed over the windshield, smearing the rain on the glass so it was even harder for her to see.

Praying, she maneuvered her car around a sharp curve. The tires squealed and shimmied with the excessive speed, and she checked the mirror again. The other vehicle stayed right with her, its high beam headlight glaring into her eyes.

It certainly wasn't safe to race through a storm at one o'clock in the morning while she was dizzy and feeling off, but she didn't want to face a killer on a deserted country road. She had no weapon. No way to defend herself. Worse, she was exhausted and was worried she wouldn't be able to stand, much less fight.

"A quarter mile to go," Delaney mumbled when

she saw the pond and cluster of cedars that marked the beginning of Cash's property.

Delaney made the final turn and sped through the cattle gates that fronted the ranch with its acres of pasture, house and outbuildings. She glanced behind her. And everything inside her went still. Because there was nothing there. No SUV. No head-lights. No one.

When her chest began to ache, Delaney released the breath that'd backed up in her lungs, and she stared into the rearview mirror. The empty dark-ness behind her should have made her feel elated and safe. It didn't.

Mercy, had she imagined that someone was fol-lowing her?

No. She couldn't have been mistaken about something like that. She just couldn't have.

Delaney slowed down and clamped her teeth over her bottom lip to keep it from trembling. Why did everything seem slightly out of focus? And wrong. Something was definitely wrong. But what? She couldn't think through the haze to try to figure it out.

More lightning veined across the sky as she came to a stop in front of Cash's place. It was dark. Not even the porch light was on. He was obviously in bed, but that wasn't unusual. He didn't keep late hours since he was usually up early to deal with the ranch-ing chores before going into the sheriff's office.

The cold spring rain pelted her when she got out of the car, but Delaney managed to make her way across the yard. Each step was an effort. She was dizzy. So dizzy. And she was soaked by the time she used her key to let herself inside the house.

She leaned against the wall and peeled off her wet dress, surprised that she wasn't wearing any underwear. It took her a moment to recall that she'd left everything but her purse at the hospital.

Yes. The hospital in Lubbock.

She'd dressed in a hurry so she could get out of there.

But why?

Because someone had wanted her dead. That was why she'd panicked when she'd seen the SUV following her. Except maybe there'd been no SUV. She shook her head again and pushed all of her questions and worries aside. The answers would come to her later after she'd rested.

She tossed her dress over the back of the chair in the living room. Drops of rain slid down her face, and she swiped at them with her equally wet forearm. Discarding her soggy shoes, she made her way down the hall to Cash's bedroom.

Delaney pushed open the door, and thanks to another slash of lightning, she was able to see him lying on his stomach in bed. He had a patchwork quilt covering the lower half of his body. The storm raged outside, the rain pounded on the tin roof, but it didn't disturb him. He looked peaceful.

Without taking her gaze off him, Delaney stepped closer. He stirred, his left hand brushing against the empty pillow next to him. *Her* pillow. Her place. Right there next to Cash.

She stood there for several moments, and despite the chill from her damp skin and the bone-weary fatigue, she just admired the view. And what a view it was. The rich black hair that swept against his neck. A solid back and shoulders that were corded with muscles he'd earned through years of hard work.

Even though Delaney couldn't quite see his angled face, she knew it was rugged, tanned and a little weathered. Not model-perfect by any stretch of the imagination, and that suited her just fine. Cash Mercer was definitely a cowboy. *Her* cowboy.

Delaney lifted the covers and slipped into bed next to him. He stirred again. Rolled to his side, and he automatically pulled her into his arms. He was warm. Solid.

And he was also naked.

"Cash," she whispered and snuggled to him.

His body slid against hers. Bare skin against bare skin. His breath brushed over her face.

Delaney leaned in and located his mouth. The taste of him jolted through her like the lightning outside. It soothed her and made her feel as if everything was right with the world. She pushed aside the SUV that had followed her, the storm, the hospital and all the other confusing thoughts that darted through her head. She was safe now and right where she belonged.

Cash made a sleepy sound of arousal just before

he deepened the kiss. He took her mouth, claiming it. The dizziness went up another notch, but at least this time she had an excuse for the whirling in her head. Cash's kisses always knocked her a little off-kilter—in a good kind of way.

She slid her hand down his chest and felt the firm muscles and the moisture that had rubbed off her own body. She gently circled his nipple with her fingertips and was rewarded when he grunted with pleasure.

"Delaney," he mumbled.

Just the sound of Cash saying her name was enough to send the fire roaring through her blood. She loved him, and she needed him.

She pulled him to her. The mattress shifted, easing him on top of her. Delaney took advantage of the new position and wrapped her legs around him.

"Cash," she murmured on a rise of breath.

Every muscle in his body went board-stiff.

He levered himself up slightly and stared down at her. Alarmed, Delaney caught on to his shoulders and tried to see his face. No such luck. The room was pitch-black, and this time the lightning didn't cooperate and give her a glimpse of his expression.

Cash's hoarse voice cut through the drone of the rain. "Delaney?"

His tone made it seem like a question. She almost laughed. *Almost.* "Who else would be climbing into your bed at one in the morning?"

He didn't answer her. She felt his heart hammer

against her chest. Hers was doing the same, and neither of them seemed to be breathing.

"Is this a joke?" he asked. Cursing, Cash rolled off her and bolted to his feet.

"What do you mean?" Delaney did some silent cursing of her own. Why was he acting like this?

"What the devil do you think I mean?" Cash grabbed a pair of boxers from the dresser and yanked them on. "What are you doing here? You're naked, for Pete's sake."

Despite the dizziness, Delaney sat up though she had to lean her back against the headboard to keep from slumping. "I wanted to see you."

"Why?" And it wasn't exactly a carnal invitation, either. It was more like a challenge.

A wave of panic started to crawl up her spine. "I've been sick, Cash." She almost told him about the SUV that had followed her but decided that could wait. They apparently had more important things to work out. "I was in the hospital."

"Hell." He added some raw profanity under his breath. "Why didn't you say that right off? Why were you in the hospital?"

"An allergic reaction to some meds." And there was more, but she was too tired to get into that now. "I'll feel better after I've had a good night's sleep."

"Sure." Cash scrubbed his hand over his face. "I'll make up the bed in the spare room for you." He started out the door.

"Wait. The spare room? Why would you want me to stay there?"

He slowly turned back around to face her. This time the lightning did its job. It slashed through the sky and gave her a glimpse of his face, and the bewildered expression on it. "You have something else in mind?"

Yes, she did. "We're engaged, Cash. I didn't figure you'd have any objections if we slept together. What's the matter with you anyway?"

"Engaged?" he spat out. Then he went still, the silence hanging in the air for several long moments. "What the heck are you talking about?"

That panic turned into a full-fledged roar. The muscles in her stomach tightened. Her breath became thin. "What's wrong?"

"You tell me, Delaney. I don't know where you got the idea that we're engaged. We're not. In fact, I haven't seen you in over a year."

No.

That wasn't true. It couldn't be true.

But she couldn't get the words of denial to leave her mouth. Almost terrified at what she might see, Delaney reached over and turned on the lamp. She didn't dare look at Cash. Not yet. Instead, she glanced down at her left hand.

There was no engagement ring on her finger. Nothing. Not even a faint line to indicate that it had ever been there.

A ragged groan tore from her throat. "Oh, God."

Chapter Two

All Cash could manage to say was another "hell."

Delaney sure had a way of capturing his complete attention, but in this case, that wasn't a good thing. A year ago, it would have pleased him bigtime if Delaney had shown up in the middle of the night and crawled naked into his bed. But not tonight. Something was wrong.

He walked to the bed and pressed the back of his hand to her forehead. No fever. His gaze met hers, and in the depths of those cat green eyes, he saw a whole lot of confusion and panic. Of course, he hadn't needed to look into her eyes to realize that. She was clearly disoriented.

Cash studied her milky complexion. She was too pale, and there were dark circles beneath her eyes. Even though he'd been half-asleep when he kissed her, he hadn't detected any alcohol on her breath. No. She wasn't drunk, but that was one of the few things he could rule out.

"I'll call the doctor," he let her know.

He reached for the phone, but Delaney caught his arm. "Please don't. Not yet. Things are...sort of whirling around in my head. Just give me a minute to catch my breath, and I'll be all right."

Cash didn't think a minute would help much of anything for her. Nor would simply catching her breath. Whatever was wrong with her was no doubt serious.

"What kind of allergic reaction did you have that landed you in the hospital?" he asked.

Delaney glanced down at the plastic hospital bracelet strapped on her wrist. "It was to some pain meds."

Cash bit off some profanity. "And they discharged you like this, while you're still out of it?"

"No." A tear slid down her cheek. She didn't even seem aware of it and didn't try to wipe it away. "I'd been in the hospital for days. At least I think it was days." She paused, her forehead bunching up. "But I wasn't discharged. I left on my own because I was scared."

His concern went into overdrive. "Scared? Of what?"

Delaney shifted her gaze to his, and she hugged the quilt to her body. "We're really not engaged?"

This wasn't a conversation he wanted to have now, but it was probably best not to put it off. He'd consider this groundwork and then he could get answers about that hospital stay.

"No," he said, trying to keep any trace of emotion out of his voice. "We were engaged a while back, but we broke things off about a year ago."

"Sweet heaven." Delaney started to cry in earnest, the tears spilling from her eyes.

Cash considered reaching for her, but she moved farther away from him. And he let her. She seemed to be coming to terms with a whole bunch of stuff. The broken engagement, yes, but also why she'd come to his house in the middle of the night.

"I remember now," she said through the broken sobs. "I remember. We argued a lot about my father. I left because I didn't think we could work out things."

Yeah. And that about summed up their entire four-month-long engagement. Delaney and he had spent hours, maybe even days, arguing about her father, Gil, a small-time rancher who hadn't wanted his little girl getting together with the likes of Cash. That was because Gil blamed Cash's father, Sheriff Jeb Mercer, for tearing his family to pieces. Gil hadn't been shy about voicing his objections as often as he got a chance, along with pressuring Delaney to end things.

Delaney had caved.

And until tonight Cash hadn't seen her since she'd handed him back the engagement ring and told him it was over between them.

Delaney drew his attention back to her when she draped the quilt around her shoulders and started to get off the bed. "I'll just be going."

"I don't think so." He stopped her from getting up. "You're staying put. I'll call my doctor and see if he'll make a house call. If not, I'll drive you to the Clay Ridge Hospital."

"No," she insisted, and her response was loud and fast. "I don't want anyone to know where I am. Someone followed me, Cash. I saw the headlights in my rearview mirror when I was driving out here."

Cash eased down on the bed next to her. He hated the fear he heard in her voice, and he hated even more that he didn't know if there was a real reason for it or not. After all, she'd thought they were still engaged. Maybe the person following her was just part of the disorientation caused by the allergic reaction.

"Look, the person behind you on the road was probably one of Matt O'Brien's boys," Cash explained. He kept his tone calm, hoping it would calm her as well. "They're always out late at night."

She frantically shook her head. "It wasn't one of Matt's sons. I swear it wasn't."

Because she seemed on the verge of panicking, he slid his arm around her. "You got a good look at the person?"

"No. But this isn't the first time he's followed me. It's been going on for a while now. Weeks."

Hell. Weeks. If that was true, then no wonder she was terrified. "You've let the police in Lubbock know about this?" Since he'd heard that was where Delaney lived these days, that would be the thing to do.

"They know," she assured him.

There was nothing uncertain about that response. He checked her eyes. They seemed clearer than they had been just minutes earlier, and she no longer seemed as confused.

"Why would this person be following you?" he asked.

Delaney hesitated. For a moment. Then two. "He wants me dead."

Cash had braced himself for her to say almost anything. Not that, though. He battled to keep his emotions in check, but it wasn't easy to do after hearing that.

"Start from the beginning," he insisted. "Tell me about this man you believe wants you dead."

He could tell she was doing her best to try to compose herself. And she failed. Cash didn't miss the tremble of her bottom lip or the soft shudder of her breath. She managed to assemble a veneer to mask her fear—and whatever else she was feeling—but that veneer looked ready to crumble at any moment.

Delaney moistened her lips. "Last year, when I was still working as a public defender, I was given a manslaughter case. The victim was a young woman who was killed during a domestic dispute."

It didn't take long for Cash to flip back through his memory. That'd happened shortly before Delaney had broken off their engagement. "I remember. You were pretty stressed out about it."

"Yes, I was." Her words were deliberate, as if

she were choosing them carefully. "The defendants were brothers—Webb and Ramone Bennison. Even though they had separate trials, I was the attorney for both of them. Webb was accused of manslaughter for killing the woman, Beatrice Stockwell, who was his live-in lover. Ramone was charged as an accomplice."

Cash tried to keep the knot from tightening in his stomach. He knew all of this already. Knew that she had been a public defender in Lubbock. She'd gotten the job right out of law school when she was barely twenty-four. Neither her father nor Cash had approved of the move, but Delaney had been determined to do a job that she thought would make a difference. After all, she'd said, everyone deserved to have a good lawyer.

But Cash knew there was a lot more to it than that.

Guilt and blame were greedy monsters that could suck the life right out of you. He had firsthand knowledge of that. He'd failed to keep his kid brother safe, and as a result, Joe had been kidnapped as a toddler and never seen again.

Delaney felt the guilt, too, but hers had a whole different twist to it. When she was sixteen, her father had walked in on her date, Aaron Skyler, trying to rape her. Gil had gone after the boy.

And in a blind rage, Gil had killed him with blows from a baseball bat.

That had led to Gil's arrest by none other than

Cash's father, Sheriff Jeb Mercer. Jeb had charged Delaney's father with excessive force resulting in manslaughter since he'd outweighed the boy and Aaron hadn't been armed. In fact, Aaron hadn't even fought back and had been trying to run out of the house when Gil had confronted him.

The charges had been controversial. So had the conviction, and Gil had gotten some jail time. He had also ended up losing his ranch. Added to that, after his release, Gil had needed several stays in rehab as well as mental health facilities when depression had taken over.

"Webb Bennison was my first manslaughter case," Delaney continued a moment later. He saw her mouth tremble again and barely resisted the urge to pull her closer. "And I lost it."

"Because Webb was guilty," Cash quickly pointed out.

She lifted her shoulder but then nodded. "There was a lot of evidence against him. Still, Webb thought I could have done a better job of defending him."

"You couldn't have," he assured her.

She made a sound as if she didn't quite buy that. "Maybe, but Webb was convicted. His brother, Ramone, was acquitted. Webb went to jail, but three weeks ago he escaped during a routine transfer. It was some kind of paperwork mix-up. They literally let him walk out of there."

This time Cash didn't manage to bite off the

profanity. Damn it. He hadn't heard about Webb's escape, but then Webb had never lived in Cash's jurisdiction. He wouldn't have gotten any kind of alert for it.

As soon as he got Delaney settled in for the night, he needed to make two phone calls. One to the doctor. The other to a cop friend in Lubbock to find out everything he could about the search for Webb. No wonder she was so worried about being followed. Or killed. Webb had been a huge nightmare from the moment he'd come into Delaney's life.

Breathing out a weary sigh, Delaney pushed her fingers through her wet hair. "For a couple days after Webb's escape, I thought he was dead," she explained, her voice wavering. "The Rangers found his burned car near Marble Falls. It'd gone over one of the bluffs. They were sure he died, but I've seen him since then. Just glimpses. But I know it's Webb."

That knot in his stomach got much worse.

Telling him all of this seemed to sap what was left of her resolve. Her eyes watered, and Cash saw her blink back more tears. Again, he had to resist holding her, but that wouldn't end up being good for either of them. There was a darn good reason Delaney and he were no longer together.

Her father, Gil.

And that reason was still around in spades. It had taken Cash too long to get over the crushed heart Delaney had left him with, and he didn't want another round of that. Still, the attraction was there. And that was his cue to shift his focus back to stopping the threat.

"You're sure it's Webb Bennison who's stalking you and not his brother?" he asked.

It took her a moment to compose herself, and she finally nodded. "I'm sure. No one has seen or heard from Ramone in a while. He disappeared after his acquittal. Besides, if he'd wanted to stalk me, he wouldn't have waited all these months."

That didn't mean Cash would write the man off. Maybe both brothers were in on this.

"And then there's the letter," Delaney added. "Webb sent it last week. He said he was going to kill me. He didn't sign it," she added before he could ask. "But I'm sure it's from him."

"What exactly did the letter say?" Cash pressed.

She paused, swallowed hard. "Just that he intended to torture me, to make me pay for not doing my job." She shuttered. "The crime lab has the letter now, but I saved a copy. It's at my house in Lubbock."

He nodded. "I want to see it tomorrow. And I also want to get one of my deputies involved in the search for Webb," he informed her. Deputy Jesse McCloud was as good a cop as they came, and he would work hard to piece all of this together.

Cash tipped his head to the guest room. "Why don't you try to get some sleep? In the morning we'll figure out what to do about all of this."

Cash braced himself for Delaney to object, for her to tell him that she didn't want to wait. Or to sleep. But the objection never came. She gave a weak nod and started toward the guest room. "Thanks for everything, Cash."

"You're welcome."

He'd hardly gotten out the last syllable before she interrupted him. "But that doesn't mean I want you to pull your Cash-the-protector routine. Webb's my problem. Not yours. Now that I'm thinking clearer, I know I shouldn't have brought this to you. I shouldn't have come here."

The corner of his mouth hitched. Well, it sure hadn't taken her long to stand her ground. But then, it rarely did.

"Cash-the-protector," he repeated under his breath. So that was how Delaney thought of him and none too fondly, either, judging from her smart-mouth tone. Well, it didn't matter. He didn't need her approval to help her out with this.

He was about to turn on his security system when his phone rang. Heaven knew who was calling this late, but it probably wouldn't be good news.

"Sorry to bother you," the man said. "I'm Kevin Byers, a private detective. I work, or rather I *worked* for Delaney. You're Cash Mercer, her ex-boyfriend?"

"Yeah." He checked to make sure Delaney hadn't come out of the guest bedroom. Thankfully, the door was still closed. "Listen, Delaney's already turned in for the night. Can this wait until morning?"

"I hadn't called to speak to her anyway. I just wanted to make sure she was there and that she was all right. When I found out she'd left the hospital, I was worried about her."

There was something about the man's tone that set Cash's teeth on edge. Maybe it was plain old-fashioned jealousy. The guy certainly seemed concerned about Delaney. Concerned in a too-concerned kind of way.

"She's fine," Cash said curtly.

"Well, good. Uh, I guess you know I've been trying to find this Webb Bennison. Delaney hired me to do that, but then she fired me."

"Not a surprise if you couldn't find him," Cash grumbled.

Cash could almost see the man scowl. "No, but there's a reason why I haven't located him. Delaney doesn't have a stalker."

Now it was Cash who scowled. "She says she does."

"I know. But I'll tell you what I told her. I looked for this Webb every day for nearly three weeks, and never once laid eyes on him. In fact, no one has, including the entire Lubbock Police Department or anyone in the other law enforcement agencies searching for him."

"Delaney's laid eyes on him," Cash quickly pointed out.

There was a moment of uncomfortable silence on

the other end of the line. "So she claims, but only her. No one else. And that should tell you something."

Cash didn't know this man, but he definitely didn't like him. "What should that tell me, other than the fact the guy's been careful?"

"Webb Bennison's dead," he insisted. "Delaney's suffering from acute delirium. Did she tell you that?"

"She mentioned it." Not in those exact words, of course. But Cash had gotten the gist of it when she mistook him for her fiancé. Still, she'd quickly recovered her grasp on reality.

"The only stalker after Delaney is the one in her own imagination," Byers added. "She didn't tell you everything, did she?" he asked before Cash could say anything else.

"What the hell does that mean?" Cash countered.

From the other end of the line, Cash heard the PI drag in a long, weary-sounding breath. "Delaney wasn't just in the hospital, Sheriff Mercer. She was under psychiatric observation. And she didn't just walk out. She escaped."

Chapter Three

The sunlight stabbing through the window woke
her. Delaney forced her eyes open, but it took several hard blinks just to be able to focus. Even then
she felt as if she'd just spent the night being tossed
around on a carnival ride.

She glanced at the room. Got her bearings. And
then she groaned.

What in the name of heaven was she doing here
in Cash's spare bedroom? Delaney struggled with
the answer much as she'd struggled to focus. She
remembered leaving the hospital because she was
scared Webb Bennison was there, that he was coming after her. She'd driven to the ranch during a
bad storm…

Oh, mercy.

And then she'd stripped off her clothes and
climbed into bed with Cash. She did that while he
was naked, thinking he was still her fiancé. Worse,
they'd kissed and come within a heartbeat of making love.

Cursing herself and the fog in her head, Delaney threw back the covers. She had to find Cash because she obviously owed him both an apology and an explanation. But when she caught a glimpse of herself in the mirror, she knew that talking to him would have to wait. She didn't intend to face him while she was stark naked.

He probably thought she had lost her mind. Heck, maybe she had. Others certainly thought it was true, and it was why she'd ended up in the hospital.

Delaney rummaged through his dresser and came up with a Christmas red terrycloth robe. It was probably a gift that he'd never worn, since Cash wasn't the bathrobe type.

She washed her face in the adjoining bathroom and tried to comb some of the tangles from her shoulder-length hair. She finally gave up, located a rubber band in one of the drawers and pulled the unruly mess of curls into a ponytail. One last glimpse in the dresser mirror confirmed what she'd already guessed: she looked how she felt—hungover and horrible.

The scent of coffee greeted her when she stepped into the hallway, but Delaney came to a quick stop when she heard the serious tone of Cash's voice.

"No," he insisted. "I want Buck and Ted riding fence today. Have them call me immediately if they see anything or anyone suspicious."

Security measures. Part of her was pleased that he believed there truly was a stalker after her. Another part of her, a much larger part, hated that security measures were even necessary. She shouldn't have brought this to his doorstep.

"Jesse's coming out soon," Cash added to the person on the phone, "and if he agrees we should add more men to keep watch, we will."

Delaney had hoped her situation wouldn't seem so downright scary after a good night's sleep. However, the fear was just as bone-deep as it had been when she'd first realized that Webb was stalking her and—worse—that he'd been at the hospital at the same time she was.

Delaney walked closer to the sound of Cash's voice, stopping in the doorway of the kitchen. She glanced at the dress she'd been wearing when she'd arrived the night before—it was now dry and draped over a chair at the table. Cash had his hip leaning against the counter, and despite the intense conversation he was having, his gaze snared her right away. The long, lingering look he gave her stole her breath.

She cursed herself. Cursed him, too. She didn't need this now. An attack of raging hormones. She wasn't some teenage girl with stars in her eyes and rocks in her head. She was a grown woman with more than enough problems that she didn't have time for anything else. Especially a good, old-fashioned case of lust. And that was all there was to it, she assured herself. Lust. Any deeper feelings she'd once had for Cash were long gone. They had to be gone.

Too bad there were times like now, when her body, or her heart didn't quite believe that.

Cash was dressed in the cowboy cop mode. Jeans, a gray T-shirt, boots. His black Stetson was hanging on a peg next to the back door. Rather than stand there and continue to gawk at him, she helped herself to a cup of coffee, sat at the table and waited for him to finish his phone conversation.

"I'll let you know what Jesse says," he relayed to the person on the other end of the line. He ended the call and turned toward her. "How are you feeling?"

"Fine," she quickly answered and hoped she sounded believable.

Apparently, she failed to convince him, because he scowled at her lie. "How are you feeling?" he repeated, and this time it was more of a demand than a simple question.

Delaney took a deep breath. "I'm fine, considering that my head's pounding and I have a killer stalking me." She took a long sip of her coffee and prayed it wasn't decaffeinated. She needed all the help that she could get with this blasted headache. "By the way, I'm sorry about last night."

He just stood there and looked at her. It didn't take long for that penetrating stare to unnerve her.

"Things got mixed up a little in my head," she added.

Cash's frown deepened.

"All right, they got mixed up a lot. I had this problem with some medication. An allergic reac-

tion to a new pain pill for the bad headaches I get."
Delaney paused. "Did I tell you this already?"

Cash nodded. "But what you didn't tell me was
that you'd been under psychiatric observation and
left the hospital without telling anyone."

"Oh," she said, knowing that he was going to
want to hear a lot more than just that vague response. But Cash continued before she could get
the explanation right in her head.

"Yes, *oh*. It took me a while to get the info, but
care to know what I learned?" Cash didn't wait for
an answer. "When you collapsed on the sidewalk
outside your office in Lubbock two days ago, someone took you to the ER, where you were diagnosed
with acute delirium, brought on by sleep depriva-
tion and stress. Do you remember that?"

"Yes," Delaney admitted.

What she wouldn't admit was that she hadn't actually remembered all of that until now, until he'd
just spelled it out for her. There were still some gaps
in her memory, and it scared her spitless to think
what might be in those gaps.

"Once the ER doctors had you stable," Cash
continued, "they placed you under psychiatric observation because you were having hallucinations
and possible paranoia. You were *combative*—their
word," he emphasized. "And they believed you
could harm yourself and maybe even others."

Delaney practically jumped to her feet. "It wasn't
paranoia, and I wouldn't have harmed myself or

anybody else. And the only reason I was *combative* was because they wouldn't listen to me. Webb's stalking me. He wants to kill me." She stopped. The short fit of temper had drained her of what little energy she had. "But I understand how that could sound like paranoia."

"And the hallucinations?" he pressed.

On a sigh, she sank back down onto the chair. "I thought I saw Webb in the hospital, and I screamed for help. That was possibly a hallucination," she admitted when Cash just continued to stare at her, "but I honestly believed Webb was there. He wanted to taunt me, to let me know that he could get to me anytime he wanted."

The muscles in Cash's jaw stirred, and he sat down across from her so they were eye to eye. "The doctor who treated you wants you to go back—"

"No." Delaney didn't have to think about that, either. "Yes, there's security, but Webb could get past that. The windows are locked on the ward where I was, and if he came into my room, I'd be trapped. He's a big man, and I'd have no way to fight him off."

Delaney steeled herself up to hear Cash's argument. But he simply nodded. Then he cursed. His jaw muscles went to war with each other again.

"Your doctor who did the psychiatric evaluation said it might be a day or two before all the symptoms go away," Cash explained as if he didn't like the information any better than she did. "He also said it was vital for you to get some rest in a comfortable, nonthreatening environment."

A burst of laughter left her mouth, but it wasn't from humor. "That's impossible. Not with Webb out there." Delaney gulped down more coffee. If the caffeine was going to work, it was sure taking its sweet time. "But not to worry. I don't plan to get naked and climb into bed with you again. I'll just get dressed—thank you for drying my clothing, by the way—and then I'll drive into Lubbock and speak to the cops there."

That earned her a glare. "You're not thinking about leaving, are you?"

"No," she said honestly. "I'm not thinking about it. I *am* leaving." She kept a firm grip on her cup to keep her hands from shaking. "I can't stay, Cash. Webb might learn that I've come to your ranch. That means I've put you and everybody else around here in danger."

He huffed, tapped the badge that was lying on the counter. "I'm a cop. I'm trained to deal with danger."

"This isn't your situation to deal with," she reminded him. "If I'd been thinking straight, I never would have come here."

He made a rough sound of displeasure and crammed his hands into the pockets of his jeans, making them snugger than they already were. Something Delaney wished she hadn't noticed.

"I won't let you go," he insisted. There wasn't a shred of compromise in his tone.

Her chin automatically came up. "I don't think you have a choice."

Because she didn't want to look at his narrowed amber brown eyes, Delaney got up and walked to the window. Outside, there were a few ranch hands milling around the barns. She quickly scanned their faces to make sure Webb wasn't among them.

He wasn't.

For the moment, she was safe.

Too bad that moment couldn't last for at least a couple of weeks. She was past the just-being-weary stage and had moved on to exhaustion. That comfortable, nonthreatening environment, even though it wasn't possible for her, sounded like paradise.

"Do you think Webb will quit stalking you simply because you leave here?" Cash asked.

"No." When her fingers began to ache from the tight grip, she put her coffee cup on the counter. "But this is my problem, and I'll—"

"Wrong. It's my problem, too." He swore under his breath. "Delaney, I can't just let you walk. You're not well and you look like you're ready to fall flat on your face." Cash paused and then huffed. "Please stay."

Delaney scowled at him. How dare he *please* her. Especially now. She felt raw and vulnerable, and a *please* could cut straight through the defenses she'd put up against him. "I can't let you do this."

He stepped closer, his boots thudding against the Saltillo tiles on the floor. She gave him a hands-off scowl. Which he ignored. Cash reached out and hauled her into his arms.

"Give me some time," he whispered right against her ear. "I don't want you driving out of here while you can hardly see straight and with that monster after you. If you stay, we can possibly put an end to this, here and now."

Delaney felt her hard-fought resolve slip a considerable notch. Before she could stop it from happening, she lowered her head to his shoulder. "I'm just so tired of all of this," she confessed.

"I know." His arms tightened around her.

She managed to choke back the tears but had no idea how long she could keep them at bay. The bone-weary fatigue seemed to seep all the way to her soul. And therein lay a huge problem. She couldn't allow her fatigue and her situation to draw her closer to Cash. She just couldn't.

There was a knock at the door, and Cash immediately stepped away from her. Delaney pulled in her breath to steady herself. It didn't help. Her heart was already pounding.

"I'll see who it is," he told her. "Just wait here."

Delaney did stay put, but only because she didn't think she could convince her legs to move. Mercy, she had to get a grip.

She cursed her body, and herself, for even allowing that embrace to happen. She didn't have time or the energy to deal with an attraction to a man, any man, but especially Cash. Their history put a high price tag on physical attraction, and it was a cost that Delaney didn't want to pay again.

"I want to see her," she heard a male voice demand.

Not Webb. But she recognized the speaker. It was Kevin Byers, the private detective she'd hired.

And fired.

She hurried into the living room, where the men stood in the doorway. It was obvious from the stern look on Cash's face that he wasn't pleased with this visit. Or surprised.

"Delaney," the PI greeted. His mouth tightened when he glanced at her bathrobe. Or rather *Cash's* bathrobe. "I've been trying to reach you."

"Really? I haven't a clue why. You no longer work for me."

Byers didn't budge from his position by the door. Probably because Cash was practically blocking his path to keep him from entering any farther.

The two men were certainly a study in contrasts. Cash was dark—his complexion and hair genetic legacies from his Lipan Apache grandmother. Byers, on the other hand, had pale skin, and his hair was the color of the moon. Their clothes were a huge contrast, too. Cash might have been a cop, but beneath it, he was all cowboy in his jeans, boots and work shirt. Byers wore khakis, a crisp white shirt and aftershave so thick and musky that she smelled it all the way across the room.

Byers kept his attention firmly on her. "I had to come. And you know why, Delaney. I had to put an end to this nonsense and make sure you get some medical attention. There's no stalker after you."

She saw the muscles in Cash's jaw jump. Thankfully, he'd seen proof to the contrary. At least in a way he had. Last night, Cash had seen her terrified. Certainly that had convinced him that Webb was after her?

Well, maybe it had.

"There is a stalker," she assured Byers. But that was all the assurance she intended to give him. "I want you to go. There's no reason for you to be here."

That seemed to be the only impetus Cash needed to latch on to Byers's arm. "You're leaving. Now."

Byers held his ground and waved a sheet of paper in the air. "I have proof there's no stalker."

Cash's gaze rifled to hers. He didn't say a word, but in that look, there were questions.

"Then your so-called proof is wrong," Delaney told Byers. "Webb followed me last night. And frankly I'm a little tired of you telling me what is and isn't happening in my life. Webb's real. His threats are real."

Byers simply handed her the paper. "It's a copy of the lab report for the letter you say you received from Webb. A friend of mine at the lab managed to get the report for me."

Delaney felt a cold hard knot tighten in her stomach as she took the paper from the man. She had no idea what the report would reveal, but from the glimmer of victory in Byers's eyes, it wasn't good. After all, Byers was convinced she'd fabricated Webb and his threats.

Cash went to her side. "Do you want me to toss this guy out of here?"

"Not just yet." But she might take Cash up on his offer later. Or as riled as she was, she could do it herself.

Delaney scanned through the technical words used for the analysis until she got to the summary at the bottom. She took in the words, the impact of them nearly knocking the breath out of her.

"Oh, God," she managed.

"It's your DNA on the sealed part of the envelope," Byers provided. "It's not merely from you touching it. You licked the envelope. You sealed it. I think that says it all, don't you, Delaney?"

She shook her head. How could her DNA possibly be on that envelope? It'd been a letter from Webb. Not that he'd signed it, of course. And the threat had been veiled with comments hinting that they would get together very soon. Still, Delaney had known it was a threat.

"Delaney?" she heard Cash say. "Are you okay?"

She didn't even attempt a lie this time. "No." She handed him the report. "This isn't right. Webb sent me that letter. I swear he sent it. This report is wrong."

She must have sounded frantic, because Cash laid the report on the table and gave her a reassuring glance. There was nothing gentle, however, about the scathing look he gave Byers. "You're leaving. Do you want to walk out of here on your own, or do you need me to give you some *encouragement*?"

"I'll go," Byers assured him. "But I think you should get Delaney professional help. She's having some kind of breakdown. The cops won't be pleased when they learn she filed a bogus report."

Cash jerked open the door. "You just wore out what little was left of your welcome." He muscled his shoulder against Byers and pushed the man onto the porch. Cash slammed the door in his face.

"She needs help," Byers yelled. "Do us all a favor and make sure she gets it."

Delaney didn't release the breath she'd been holding until she heard Byers stomp off the porch and drive away. She waited. Waited for Cash to question her about the report, and her sanity. However, he didn't say a word.

"Byers thinks I belong on the psychiatric ward." Delaney squeezed her eyes shut a moment. "And after the police read that report, they'll agree with him."

"Not necessarily. It wouldn't be the first time a lab has come back with inaccurate results. We can have the envelope retested, and it'll prove what you've been saying."

Delaney replayed everything he'd just said. Cash believed her. He didn't think she'd lost her mind.

Relief rushed through her. Followed by the dread.

Was this the real reason she'd come home—because she needed someone to accept that what was happening to her was real and not just in her head?

He pushed a wispy strand of hair off her cheek. "I get the feeling there's some tension between you and the PI," he commented. "And I don't think it's because the man has seriously bad taste in after-shave." Cash made a face, fanned the air. "Might take a while to get the stench out of here."

Delaney gave a nervous laugh. "I hired him last month and then fired him nearly a week ago."

"Because he doesn't believe there's a stalker." Cash paused. "But there's more to it than that."

The man was a pro at reading her. It made her wonder why she hadn't just spilled everything before Byers had shown up. "Byers wanted a relationship. I wasn't interested, and I don't think he likes to hear no for an answer."

Cash didn't say anything for several snail-crawling moments. "You're sure it's not more than that? He seemed, well, determined to get back at you."

She heard what was beneath his words. A PI should have thicker skin. And the truth was—it had felt like more. She just wasn't sure what. Or why. But Byers's reaction to her firing him was just off.

"I knew I should have punched him," Cash grumbled when she didn't say anything.

His tone was in jest but not completely. Delaney had no trouble hearing the underlying threat. Cash would have stood up for her, and that brought her back full circle to the point she'd been trying to drill into her head. They couldn't do anything that might test, or tempt, the precarious barriers they'd built between them.

Those barriers were necessary.

For reasons she didn't want him to know. Reasons *he* couldn't know. Because then Cash would want to right that wrong, too.

Delaney took both a mental and physical step back from him. "I need to get some things from my house in Lubbock."

"I'll go with you," Cash insisted.

She didn't even try to talk him out of it. The truth was, since Cash was insistent on helping her, she really didn't want to go outside alone because Webb might still be out there. Or even Byers. But she couldn't let that possibility stop her from coming up with a plan of action.

For starters, she had to figure out a way to convince the cops in Lubbock that the threat was real. That her life was in danger. That her DNA on the envelope had been planted or something. And she had to do it fast. Despite Cash's *hospitality*, she couldn't continue to stay at the ranch and put him in danger.

She took her dress and shoes to the bathroom to put them on, only to remember that she still didn't have underwear. Something that Cash already knew since he'd obviously gotten her dress off the floor and put it in the dryer. No way would he have not noticed that there were no other items of her clothing lying around.

Delaney dressed as fast as she could and saw Cash waiting for her when she came out of the bathroom. Specifically, he was waiting and watching at the window. No doubt making sure no one was about to ambush them.

"I've alerted the ranch hands," Cash let her know. "They'll be on the lookout for Webb."

"Thank you," she said, truly grateful for his help.

But having the hands be on the lookout wasn't enough. If Webb wanted to get onto the ranch undetected, he could probably figure out a way to do it. The ranch was a big place with plenty of ways in and out.

"And you're thinking I can't help you do what's necessary to stop Webb," Cash added, looking her straight in the eyes. "But I will. Promise," he added.

Promise. That was one of his favorite words. Sometimes he said it with a slathering of sarcasm. Other times, there was enough sexual heat in it to trigger them falling straight into bed. But now it was just that. A promise. He would help her, and in doing so, he would put his life on the line.

Delaney wouldn't argue with him about that. Not now anyway. But she needed to come up with a better plan than the one that was playing out right now.

Her car was still parked out front, but Cash stopped her when she started toward it. "One of the hands checked it out, and the battery's dead," he told her. "You'd left the door open and the parking lights on when you got here."

Delaney huffed in frustration, but it didn't surprise her. She'd really been out of it the night before. It was a miracle that she'd even managed to get to the ranch.

"We'll take my truck," Cash added.

His dark blue pickup was parked in the driveway on the side of the house, and they headed in that direction. They had nearly reached it when she heard a sound.

A growl.

Delaney's gaze whipped toward the road. Just ahead, barely yards away, were five Dobermans. How they'd gotten so close without her seeing them, she didn't know, but these were no pets. They had their teeth bared.

And the dogs were already charging right at them.

Cash shoved her toward the truck, and the moment he had the passenger's-side door open, he pushed her inside. He followed her, with Delaney dragging him in, but one of the dogs snapped at his leg. He kicked at it, forcing it to move back, and Cash bolted into the cab of the truck with her. He slammed the door shut just as the other dogs lunged at them.

"Did you get bit?" she blurted out.

"No." He moved out of her grip and took out his phone. "Brent," he said when his ranch hand answered. "We've got five Dobermans in the front yard, and they're not very friendly."

"Yeah. I just got a call from one of the hands at Eagle Hill," she heard Brent say. "The dogs belong to the new owner, and they got out."

Eagle Hill was a nearby ranch, but she hadn't known there was a new owner. The place had been unoccupied the whole time she'd been with Cash.

"The owner's driving around looking for them," Brent went on, "but I'll text the hand and have them get over here ASAP."

However, before Cash could even end the call, a red truck barreled up the road and came to a quick stop. A man hurried out. He was well over six feet tall and had a bulky build. He whistled, and the dogs immediately turned and hurried to him. With a snap of his fingers, the dogs jumped into the back of the truck.

"Sorry about this," the man called out, and he started toward them.

Cash got out, facing their visitor, and Delaney stepped out behind him. Even when the man got closer, she couldn't see much of his face because of the angle of his hat, but there was something about his voice that turned her blood to ice.

Using his thumb, their visitor pushed back the brim of his hat, his gaze zooming right in on her.

"Delaney," he said, smiling.

But she definitely wasn't smiling. Delaney knew she was looking at the face of a killer.

Chapter Four

Ramone Bennison.

Cash cursed under his breath when he instantly recognized the man, and slid his hand over the gun in his shoulder holster. After all, Ramone might be a free man, acquitted of helping his brother murder a woman, but Cash wasn't at all sure the guy was innocent. Especially considering those attack dogs.

Cash also stepped in front of Delaney, but not before he felt the muscles tense in her arm.

Hell.

Seeing Ramone was no doubt like stepping back into a nightmare for her. Nightmares of the threats from Ramone's brother, Webb. Considering what had been going on recently with Delaney, those threats likely seemed even more menacing than the dogs.

Ramone shifted his attention, and then his smile, to Cash. "The gun's not necessary," he informed Cash.

Cash didn't move his hand, and he didn't buy

into Ramone's friendly tone and smile. Not with what had to be buckets of bad blood between Delaney and the man.

"What are you doing here?" Delaney demanded, and Cash had to hand it to her—she sounded a lot stronger than she probably felt.

Ramone hitched his thumb in the direction behind Cash's property. "I'm your new neighbor. I bought Eagle Hill, the old Henderson ranch."

Cash shook his head. "I was told the new owner was a guy named Frank Taylor."

"He's my business partner," Ramone quickly explained. "He bought the ranch, but I'll be running it. At least I will once I get it fixed up."

That didn't sound aboveboard. Then again, Cash figured he'd suspect any- and everything the man said or did.

"Why the hell would you buy a place so close to me?" Cash snapped. "Because I sure as hell don't believe you didn't know Delaney's connection to me."

The breath Ramone released was long and sounded weary. Of course, weariness could be faked, and Cash knew this could be some kind of sick game of cat and mouse that Ramone and Webb were playing with Delaney.

"The ranch was a good price, a good investment," Ramone said. "And yes, I knew we'd share a property line. Once I was settled in, I'd planned on coming over to let you know I have no ill will or bitter feelings for Delaney or you." He paused a heartbeat, his gaze sliding between Delaney and Cash. "Besides, last I heard Delaney and you weren't even together."

No, they weren't together, but Cash had no intention of confirming that to a man who might be out to harm her. He wanted Ramone to believe that Delaney would have all the protection she needed if Ramone and Webb came after her. And she would. Well, she'd have it from Cash anyway.

"Delaney," Ramone continued when neither Cash nor she said anything. He shifted his gaze to her. "There's no reason for you to be worried about me being here."

A burst of air left her mouth. A hollow laugh, definitely not one from humor. "Your brother wants to kill me."

Ramone lifted his shoulder in a noncommittal shrug and glanced behind him at the dogs. Maybe to make sure they were staying put. They were.

"Maybe you want to kill me, too," she added.

Ramone shook his head. "No. I don't. And FYI, I believe Webb's dead," he threw out there like gospel. "I think if he were alive, he would have already gotten in touch with me. He hasn't."

"You and I don't share the same opinion." Delaney stepped to Cash's side, no doubt so she could face Ramone head-on. "I believe Webb's taunting me and that he plans to murder me."

No shrug this time. Ramone stared at her a moment. Then he nodded. "I hope you're wrong about that. But if Webb's alive like you think, well, he'll probably be holding a grudge."

"And you're not holding one?" Cash fired back.

Ramone smiled again. "I didn't kill anyone, and I didn't help Webb kill anyone. And the jury agreed. That's why I'm a free man. So, no grudge for me, not toward either of you." His smile faded, and he shrugged. "As for my brother, things weren't solid between us after the trial. You could say I'm having a little trouble forgiving him for dragging me into the mess that landed him in jail."

Cash didn't believe that for a second. Blood was blood, and yeah, he personally didn't have that kind of connection with his own kin, but he thought that Ramone and Webb might still be tight.

Ramone sighed as if frustrated by what he believed Cash was thinking, and then he tipped his head to the dogs. "I'd best be getting them back. Sorry about the Dobermans getting out. They're all bark, no bite, but I'm sure it was...unsettling." He seemed to savor the word. "It won't happen again."

"It'd better not," Cash snapped, and he made sure that sounded like a warning from a cop. "Because if they get out again, I'll come after you. That's a promise." The last bit was much more than a warning. It sounded very much like the threat that it was.

Cash gave Ramone a hard stare until the man drove away, and then he got Delaney back in the truck. He'd already had plenty of concerns about this drive into Lubbock, but dealing with Ramone skyrocketed those concerns.

"Please don't tell me I have no reason to be worried," Delaney muttered. "Because I'm not buying that it's a coincidence that Ramone bought the ranch as a good investment."

Cash wanted to try to reassure her that all would be well, but he didn't want her wearing rose-tinted glasses. Not for something like this. Rather, he wanted her to stay alert and focused. Like now. As he drove away from the ranch, both of them glanced around to make sure they weren't being followed.

Or about to be attacked.

"I'll keep an eye on Ramone," he assured her. "And I'll check on the sale of the ranch. If there's anything, and I mean anything, off about it, I'll use it to file charges against him."

He got that started by pressing the button on his steering wheel to make a quick, hands-free call to his office, and Jesse answered on the first ring.

"Ramone Bennison just showed up at my place," Cash told his deputy. "He claims he bought the old Henderson ranch."

Jesse muttered some profanity, his voice pouring through the truck. "You think Webb's there with him?"

"Maybe, but if he is, I'm betting he'll keep his sorry butt well hidden. Ramone had to know that once word got out about him being the owner, then anybody in law enforcement would look at it as a possible hiding place for Webb."

But Cash immediately rethought that. Maybe law enforcement wouldn't look because they thought Webb was dead.

"What do you need me to do?" Jesse asked.

"Contact the Texas Rangers and tell them about Ramone. Then dig into the sale of the property and into any paperwork you can get your hands on. If there's dirt to find, I want it found." He could use that dirt ASAP to get the man out of Clay Ridge.

"Will do," Jesse answered. "You want me to see if I can set up some kind of surveillance in case Webb is at the ranch?"

Cash considered how to go about that. "Yeah. Arrange for security cameras, but keep them on my property so we don't have to get a warrant. There are a couple of spots where you should be able to get a visual of Ramone's house."

"Thank you," Delaney murmured.

There was no need for her gratitude. Even if Delaney and he hadn't had a history together, he would have wanted to keep an eye on Ramone. Anyone who'd been charged with such a serious crime would automatically be on his radar.

Cash had just ended his conversation with Jesse when his phone rang, and he frowned when he saw the name of the caller on the dash screen of his truck. Leigh as in Leigh Mercer. She was not only his sister, but she was also sheriff of the nearby town of Dark River.

Most brothers probably weren't surprised to get calls from their siblings, but the two of them weren't exactly close, and she rarely had reason to get in touch with him.

"A problem?" Cash said the moment he answered.

"Is Delaney with you?" Leigh immediately said.

Of all the questions he'd thought his sister might ask, that hadn't been one of them. Leigh knew Delaney, of course. They'd all grown up together in Dark River, but like Cash, Delaney had moved away when she turned eighteen.

"I'm here," Delaney volunteered. And Cash was glad she had. It would signal Leigh not to say anything sensitive about an investigation in case his sister was calling cop to cop.

Leigh muttered something he didn't catch, but he didn't have to hear exactly what she'd said to pick up on the frustrated tone. That probably had something to do with his and Leigh's last visit.

Shortly after Cash's breakup with Delaney.

After getting many nudges and calls from their father and friends, Leigh had drawn the short straw and come to Cash's house to check on him. He'd been surly and on his way to getting drunk. In other words, not his finest hour, and Leigh might be making sure he wasn't about to have a repeat of that.

"How'd you know I was with Delaney?" he came out and asked his sister.

"I just got a visit from a PI," Leigh explained. "Kevin Byers."

Cash wasn't sure whose groan was louder—his or Delaney's. "I fired him," Delaney said. "And he's not happy about it."

"Yeah, I picked up on that right away." Leigh paused. "Any truth to what Byers said? Because he's claiming that you escaped from a mental hospital and that you need help. Help that Byers doesn't believe Cash will give you because you've convinced him that you're right as rain."

Now Cash cursed. "Byers shouldn't have gotten into all of that with you."

"Agreed. But he did. He said since Delaney grew up here in Dark River and he knew we'd been friends that I might have some influence over her."

"Influence to do what exactly?" Cash snarled. "Get Delaney to turn herself over to him?"

"Yes. He thought I'd be willing to talk her into it. Of course, I have no intentions of doing that. And while I don't want to poke my nose where it doesn't belong, I'm calling to ask if there's any way I can help."

For an instant, Cash got a flash of Leigh and him as kids. They hadn't been close even then. Too many bad memories and family turmoil for that. But even with the turmoil, Leigh had usually been on his side. And vice versa.

"Does anyone in the crime lab owe you any favors?" Cash asked. "Because I need a letter retested."

"The letter that Webb sent Delaney?" Leigh quickly provided. That was also info she'd no doubt heard from the PI.

"That's the one," Cash verified. "I believe Webb sent it, but according to Byers, Webb's DNA wasn't on it. Only Delaney's."

"All right," Leigh agreed a moment later. "I'll call in some favors. By the way, after I explained to Byers that I wouldn't help him, that anything Delaney might have done isn't even in my jurisdiction, he said with or without my help, he intended to have her arrested for making a false claim and manufacturing evidence."

"That's not gonna happen," Cash snapped.

Because an arrest could get her killed. If he couldn't legally stop Delaney from being taken, then he'd do it illegally. That'd make him an outlaw, a maverick, but it'd be damn worth being on the wrong side of the badge to keep her alive.

"I'll go ahead and call the lab guys so they can get started on the letter right away," his sister said. She paused again but continued before Cash could thank her. "Something's wrong with Jeb."

Cash felt his chest tighten. Then again, that was his usual reaction to hearing his father's name. The fact that both his sister and he called him Jeb instead of *Dad* or *Father* pretty much said it all. Yeah, that family turmoil was a mess that had lasting effects, and at the center of that turmoil was Jeb.

"Define *wrong*," Cash insisted.

"He needs heart surgery. And no, I don't have the details because Jeb won't give them to me. You know how he is," she added in a mumble. "I just thought I should tell you."

Cash did indeed know how Jeb could be. Until his recent retirement, Jeb had been the sheriff of Dark River for over forty years. He'd been *the* law in Lubbock County. Jeb had also doled out that law with a hard hand and very little compassion.

Even when it came to his own kids.

Cash knew that Jeb still resented the hell out of him for not staying in Dark River to take over as sheriff. No way though would Cash have stayed under Jeb's thumb. But Leigh had.

Well, sort of.

She'd stayed and been elected sheriff after Jeb's retirement. It didn't matter that she was darn good at the job, either, because Jeb had made it clear that he'd wanted that particular badge to go to one of his sons. Either Cash or Joe, the son who'd been kidnapped as a toddler. Jeb had always held out hope that Joe was not only alive but that also someday he'd return and take over the reins of the law in Dark River.

And just like that, Cash got sucked back into more memories of the shambles that'd once been his life.

He cursed and wasn't able to keep that profanity to himself. Some of the words flew right out of his mouth. Leigh obviously knew how he felt, because she made a sound of agreement. She probably got sucked into the memories a lot since she was right there, right in the mix with Jeb, in Dark River.

"I'll let you know if I find out anything else about Jeb. And I'll make that call to the lab," Leigh said, clearly changing the subject.

"Thank you," Delaney spoke up. "I'm sorry about Byers bothering you. I'll call him and demand he back off."

"No need," Leigh assured her. "I told him that myself. Stay safe," she added before she ended the call.

"Are you okay?" Delaney immediately asked him.

"Yeah." Cash took a moment, hoping that moment would make him seem more okay than he was feeling. When that didn't work, he just shoved it all aside. Something he was used to doing. Dealing with any kind of news about Jeb often required shoving things aside.

"You understand complicated relationships with fathers," Cash threw out there.

"Yes," she agreed in a whisper.

Delaney kept her attention out the window. Specifically, on the side mirror where she'd be able to see anyone following them, but Cash had heard the soft sigh she released. Not a sigh of regret. Just resignation.

"Things are the same between Jeb and you?" she asked.

"Pretty much." Cash wasn't sure he should re-open this particular can of worms, but he went with it anyway while he took the exit to her house. "How about you? How are things between Gil and you?"

"Pretty much the same," she echoed. Delaney tore her attention from the side mirror to give him a long look. "My father doesn't know about the trouble I've been having. Or that I was in the hospital. I need to keep it that way."

Cash thought about that for a moment. "There's little to no chance he'd hear it from me, but Byers might contact him."

She groaned, shook her head. "After I pack some things at my house, I'll pay a visit to Byers and warn him to stay out of my business."

Cash would be making that visit with her, and if necessary, he'd use the badge to get the PI to back off. Byers had no official reason to be involved in Delaney's life. At least no reason that Cash knew of, and what the man was doing was a form of stalking.

Which brought him to his next concern.

What with her recent health scare, and with Webb, Ramone and now Byers causing her some grief, Cash didn't want Delaney trying to fix this on her own.

"Are you going to argue with me about staying at my place?" Cash came out and asked.

She opened her mouth, closed it and groaned again. "I don't want to put you in the middle of this. Plus, there's my father," she added before he could tell her the middle was exactly where he wanted to be.

Cash tried not to let that feel like a sucker punch. But it did. Always would. "You don't want Gil to know you'd be staying with me, even if it was to keep you out of harm's way?" Oh, yeah. There was plenty of bitterness in his tone.

"I don't want him to know about the harm's way," she emphasized. "It'll be easier all around if I find some other place to stay."

Well, hell. She was going to argue with him about that after all.

"I can stay with my father," Delaney added.

Once Cash got past the second sucker punch—this time of annoyance—he decided that maybe this was for the best. Not her going to her father but not wanting to stay with him. After all, Delaney clearly didn't want to get involved with him again, and that meant he'd be a fool to create a situation where they'd be under the same roof.

While she was packing her things, he'd make some calls and see about getting her into protective custody. He'd find someone who'd be willing to bend whatever laws were necessary to keep her from being arrested or killed. She needed to be with someone who knew how to keep her safe. That would get her out of Webb's path. Byers's, too.

And out of his own path as well.

Because there were other memories, too. Memories of Delaney naked in his bed. Memories that could end up causing him to make another huge mistake by giving in to the heat. Best to cool down that heat some by going with the "out of sight, out of mind" approach.

Mentally repeating that reminder and hoping it would soon sink in, Cash turned onto Delaney's street. Definitely not out in the sticks as his place was. This was a neighborhood of homes that had been built in the 1920s and then remodeled over the years.

In Delaney's case, the dark gray Craftsman-style house with the white shutters and pristine yard had once belonged to her grandmother. Delaney loved the place. When they'd gotten engaged, she'd told him that she would keep the house and maybe turn it into her law office.

Cash hadn't objected to her plans for merging their lives. After all, her work was here in Lubbock, and it wouldn't have been a long commute to the ranch, so it was a good plan. A plan that had gone to hell in a handbasket when Delaney decided to bend to her father's demands.

And that was yet something else he needed to push aside.

Cash pulled to a stop in her driveway and had a look around. Not an ordinary look but rather one where he was searching for any signs of Webb. But there was nothing. In fact, the street was empty, and he certainly didn't see anyone lurking in any of the yards.

He got out and walked to the passenger's side so he'd be right next to Delaney as they made their way up the porch. Again, there were no signs of trouble here and nothing seemed out of place.

"I need to disengage the security system," she said, taking out her phone. She frowned, though, when she pulled up the app for the controls for the system. "It's off. Not just the system, but the locks are off, too."

Cash had a look for himself and saw the red X where there should have been a green dot. "How long has it been since you've been here?" he asked.

She hesitated, shook her head. "Before I was put in the hospital."

So a couple of days. "Maybe you forgot to turn it on when you left," Cash suggested. The allergic reaction to the meds could have played into that happening. No way had she been thinking straight when she'd gone to his place and climbed into bed with him.

"I don't forget to do that. I mean, it's automatic, like putting on a seat belt. I use the app to lock the door and set the alarm." She looked at him, her eyes pleading for him to believe that. "Other than last night when I left the hospital, I've been careful because of Webb. I didn't want him to be able just to walk in."

Yeah, he got that, but she certainly hadn't been careful last night. She could have been so disoriented that she'd forgotten even something that was rote. It could be something as simple as that, but he still stepped in front of her when she reached for the door.

"Let me open it," he insisted, drawing his gun.

Her eyes widened, but she gave a shaky nod. He considered having her wait in his truck while he went inside and checked out the place, but that had its risks, too. If Webb was truly trying to get to her, he would likely try it when she was alone. That included when she might be in a vehicle by herself.

Cash glanced over his shoulder, just to make sure they weren't about to be ambushed, and he tested the knob. Definitely unlocked. With his gun ready, he stayed positioned in front of Delaney and eased open the door. And the moment he saw the foyer wall, he knew that all was not well.

There, painted in red, was a warning that turned his blood to ice.

Delaney, there's no place for you to hide. Sooner or later, I will get to you.

Chapter Five

Delaney would have staggered back a step had Cash not caught her arm to steady her. In the same motion, he shifted her behind him and lifted his gun while his gaze darted all around the foyer and to the rooms beyond.

"Webb," she said on a rise of breath. Delaney looked, too. Because she had no doubt who'd left that threatening message. No one else hated her enough to leave something like that.

Delaney, there's no place for you to hide. Sooner or later, I will get to you.

"If I'd come home last night instead of going to your place…" she muttered, but she didn't finish that. No need for her to spell out that Webb could have had her then and there. As dizzy and disoriented as she'd been, she wouldn't have been able to fight him off.

"Stay right next to me," Cash instructed. "We'll go back to the truck so I can call this in."

"You're not going to look through the house for

Webb?" she asked. Not that she wanted him to do that. No. She didn't want Cash to run into Webb, who could be lying in wait.

"Not now. If Webb's here, I don't want to take him on while you're with me."

The thought of that terrified her. Because Webb might be the one who did the *taking*. If Webb was still inside, he could kill Cash, and it would be a bonus for him, a way of getting in another jab at her to murder someone who'd been such an important part of her life.

"You need backup before you go through the house," she insisted, and Delaney would hold him to that. She wouldn't let him do the search alone.

"Let's go," Cash insisted.

With his gun still ready, he backed out of the house, adjusting his position every step so he could keep watch and continue to use his body to shield her. She kept watch, too, but didn't see anyone. However, she did hear something. The sound of an approaching vehicle.

Cash must have heard it as well, because he pivoted fast, taking aim in the direction of the sound while he pressed her back against the front exterior wall. She felt his muscles brace, preparing for what might be a fight. Delaney tried to do the same. She might not have a gun, but she had no intention of just standing there if Webb came for her.

Part of her welcomed a showdown with the snake who'd turned her life upside down. Because maybe Cash and she would be able to end the danger. Maybe it would all finally come to a stop.

She released the breath that was causing her lungs to ache when she saw the truck that pulled into her driveway. Not Webb. "It's my father," she muttered at the same time that Cash spat out, "Gil."

Cash grumbled something else that she didn't catch, but she was betting it was profanity. Her father was likely grumbling the same words, too, because he was scowling when he stepped from the truck. A scowl no doubt meant for Cash.

As usual, Gil was wearing jeans and a work shirt. Emphasis on *work* since he was a hand at a ranch just outside of Lubbock. His boots were scuffed. His cowboy hat, more than a little battered. Both were items that Delaney had offered to replace many times over, but he'd always refused.

Also as usual, she felt the mix of emotions at seeing him. The love she felt for him. And the guilt. Both were equally strong, but most times, like now, it was the guilt that won out and consumed her. Just as it was consuming him.

Before that night nearly a decade ago, her father had been a ranch owner. It hadn't been especially big, but it'd been profitable. More importantly, it'd been in his family for generations. And afterward, after he'd killed because of her, he'd become the shell of the man she saw walking toward her now. There were things that she wished she could go back and change, but that fateful night was at the top of her list.

"What's wrong?" her father asked, shifting his attention to her. "Why are you with Cash?"

Delaney had a quick debate about how much to tell him. The full truth would worry him. Maybe *more* than worry him. But it would be hard to keep this sort of thing from him. Best to fill him in on the basics and go from there.

"I'm with Cash because it would have been too risky for me to come here alone. Webb broke into my house and left me a message," Delaney said. She tried to tamp down her fear, but it was still there, as bright and glaring at the message Webb had left her. "Cash was about to call it in to the local cops."

Her father froze in midstep, his scowl morphing to one of concern. "Are you okay?"

Obviously, Cash knew the question wasn't meant for him, because he went ahead and called Lubbock PD. He made it quick, and all the while he continued to keep watch.

There was a good reason for that.

Webb could use her father's arrival as a distraction to try to gun them down. Of course, any bullets that flew right now would have a much greater chance of hitting Cash and her father than her since both of them were obviously trying to keep her covered.

"The cops will be here in about ten minutes," Cash relayed to her.

"Dad, you should go," Delaney told him. "I'll call you once they've finished searching the house."

Gil didn't hesitate. "I'm not leaving." Not a trace of a scowl remained, and his forehead bunched up in worry.

She sighed and tried to think up an argument that she could use to get him to go. But Delaney knew there wasn't one. If she mentioned the possibility of an attack from Webb, that would only make him dig in his heels even more. She hadn't seen traces of the rage her father had had when he'd killed Aaron Skyler, and she didn't want to risk bringing that to the surface again. If her father went looking for Webb, he just might find him.

And Webb might kill him.

Webb wasn't a teenage boy who could be easily beaten down. He was big and strong. And mean. Her father would be no match for the man.

"What'd the message say?" Gil insisted.

Again, she debated what to say and what tone to use. "It was just a taunt," she settled for saying, and she kept her voice level. "Something that he knew would rattle me."

It had worked, too. All the nerves in her body seemed to be firing just beneath her skin. Something that she prayed her father wouldn't be able to tell. She needed this part of the situation defused so she could concentrate on finding Webb and stopping him. She couldn't do that if she was worried about her father.

"A taunt," Gil repeated like profanity, and he paused so long that Delaney thought he might demand to know the exact words that Webb had used. He didn't. "I'm worried about you," he continued a moment later. "You were in the hospital and didn't even tell me."

Delaney groaned because she so didn't want to have this conversation now, but she also didn't want it to come down to Cash trying to force her father to leave. "How'd you find out?"

"A better question would be why I didn't hear it from you," her father argued. Except there wasn't much of an argument in his tone. However, there was hurt. Loads and loads of it.

Because Delaney could see and feel that hurt and his concerns about her, she softened her voice. "I didn't tell you because I didn't want you to worry. How'd you find out?" she repeated.

"A PI you'd hired called me," he said after hesitating.

Great. Just great. No way could she tamp down her temper this time. Byers was at it again, and that gave her another slam of anger. She was definitely going to have a conversation with the man.

"Byers also told me you were at Cash's," her father went on. "Since you weren't answering your phone, I was going to leave you a note. I figured sooner or later, you'd have to come home."

She wasn't answering her phone because she'd left it when she'd sneaked out of the hospital the night before. Delaney had taken her purse, but her phone hadn't been in it. Apparently, someone on the staff had taken it when she'd been placed under observation.

"Why'd you go to Cash and not me?" Gil asked, and yes, the hurt had gone up some significant notches. "He's Jeb Mercer's son," he said as if that were the ultimate insult.

Which, to her father, it was.

Cash cursed. "I had nothing to do with being his son, and FYI, Jeb and I aren't exactly in a cozy father-and-son relationship."

"You've got his blood," her father fired back. No hurt now. This was anger, his usual reaction when it came to Jeb or anyone in the Mercer gene pool.

"And so what? That means I'll arrest some guy for going after the SOB who tried to rape his teen-age daughter?" Cash shook his head, muttered more profanity. "I'm a lot of things, Gil, but I'm not Jeb Mercer."

Gil kept his gaze nailed to Cash. "The Mercers ruined me," he accused, his voice trembling now. "I shouldn't have gone to jail for what I did. I shouldn't have lost nearly everything I loved, and every time I see one of them, it brings back all those bad memories."

She knew he wasn't lying about the memories being bad. She'd heard his shouts when he was caught up in a nightmare and had watched him try to push back the darkness by drinking until he passed out.

And it was all her fault.

Gil scrubbed his hand over his face before he dragged in a shaky breath and looked at Delaney. "I need you to come home with me."

She couldn't do that, couldn't give Webb a reason to go after her at her father's place. "I'll be staying with a friend," she said. "Not Cash," she added when Gil's gaze shifted to Cash. "I'll be all right."

Her father studied her expression as if trying to suss out if what she'd said was true. Part of it was. But the "I'll be all right" wasn't anywhere close to being a certainty. The message left for her on the foyer wall was proof of that. If Webb could get past her security system to do that, then he would continue to come at her.

"I can't go through this again," her father muttered, and then he clamped his teeth over his bottom lip as if he hadn't meant to say that.

Delaney went to him and pulled him into a hug. "I'm sorry—"

"Don't." He moved out of her grip and backed away from her. "I can't go through this again."

She didn't try to touch him again, but Delaney did study his eyes. "Do you mean you can't deal with Cash and me? Because if so, I'm not with him."

The corner of Gil's mouth lifted in a dry smile. One that was touched with venom when his attention drifted toward Cash. "I can't watch this happen."

"Delaney is right," Cash said on a frustrated huff. "We're not together."

But he was talking to the air because her father had already turned and stormed back to his truck. She watched as he sped out of her driveway and took off down the road.

Delaney wanted to go after him, to tell him he was wrong, but mercy, she was too tired to deal with her father right now. Soon, though, she'd need to go see him and try to smooth things over. But not until she was sure that she wouldn't be bringing danger right to his doorstep.

"We need to wait in the truck," Cash reminded her. "You shouldn't be out in the open like this."

Because she knew that was true, Delaney hurried to the truck with him, and once they were inside, he motioned for her to lower herself to the seat. She did but frowned when he didn't do the same.

"You're not getting down," she pointed out.

"Because I have no intention of letting Webb sneak up on us." He stopped, shook his head. "But he'd be an idiot to do that. If he's watching the place, he'd know that I've already called for backup. My guess is that he's long gone."

Yes, but she doubted Webb had gone far. Maybe he was with his brother in Clay Ridge, where he could take the time to plot how to keep tormenting her. If so, then she hoped Webb would be caught by the security cameras that Cash's deputy was setting up. Then Cash could arrange to go in and have both Ramone and him arrested.

However, Webb could go elsewhere, and the reminder of that slammed into her.

"Webb might try to get to me through my dad," she blurted out. Delaney nearly sprang off the seat, but Cash eased her right back down.

"I was going to ask Lubbock PD to offer Gil protection. Anyone else Webb could use to try to lure you out?"

Delaney silently cursed that she hadn't already gone over all of this. "My assistant, Melanie Adams."

In fact, she needed to contact Melanie and fill her in on what was happening. Melanie often worked from home, where she lived with her parents and two younger siblings, but that didn't mean Webb couldn't find a way around them.

"Melanie Adams," Cash repeated as if picking through his memory. "I remember meeting her shortly after you hired her. I'll ask for protection for her, too. And you, of course." He paused, glanced down at his phone when it dinged with a text message.

He frowned, then cursed.

"Webb," he snarled, getting her attention.

He showed her the text he'd just gotten from an unknown caller. If you want to find me, go to Delaney's house. I left something that oughta give her a nightmare or two.

Delaney felt another wave of fear slide over her. "Webb," she agreed.

Cash continued to frown. "The text was delayed. The person sent it over an hour ago."

She'd had that happen a couple of times, especially on drives from Lubbock to Clay Ridge, and it made her wonder when Webb, or someone he'd hired, had broken in and left that message. The paint smell had still been strong, so maybe it'd happened right before he'd sent the text.

"If the text hadn't been delayed, I would have left you at my ranch and come here with a couple of local cops," Cash muttered. "So why wouldn't Webb have wanted you to see the message for yourself?"

Good question, and Delaney didn't like the possible answer. "Maybe Webb wants to get me away from you because he thinks it'll be easier to kill me that way."

Cash made a sound of agreement. "You told your father you'd be staying with a friend. You told me you'd be staying with him. Where exactly are you planning on going?"

She opened her mouth but had to close it. Because she didn't have an answer for that. Not yet anyway.

"I get it," Cash continued when she didn't say anything. "You're worried about Webb having a go at me."

Yes, but it was more than a worry. It was a fear that was already eating away at her. Webb had killed once, and given the chance, he would again.

"I can take care of myself," he assured her. "And I can make sure your father's taken care of, too. Promise."

She had no doubts, none, that Cash would do that. But it would come with a huge price tag. A price tag that he wouldn't want, but it would be there. Because she would owe him for protecting her, and even more, she would owe him for the heat that would grow because of the two of them being thrown together like this. She could already feel the pull of the strong attraction between them. And she couldn't push away just how much she wanted to be in his arms.

But it couldn't happen.

If it did, she'd have another layer of guilt in her life. Because if she was with Cash, it could cause her father to try to kill himself. Again. She'd already cost him way too much, and she couldn't risk him losing his life.

Delaney was about to explain to Cash that she would indeed make some calls. She would arrange for security for both her father and her as well as finding a safe place for both of them to stay. But she didn't get the chance to do that because of the black-and-white patrol car that turned into her driveway.

Cash huffed, likely because he'd wanted to hear what she had been about to say, and he holstered his gun before he opened his truck door. "Stay put," he warned her. "They'll have to talk to you, but I want that to happen at the police station."

So did she, and maybe the Lubbock cops would believe her when she insisted that Webb Bennison was responsible for this.

Cash stepped out, shut the truck door and made it just one step before all hell broke loose.

The blast ripped through her house.

Chapter Six

One second Cash was standing, and the next moment, he was flying through the air. He landed hard, the pain shooting through his chest and jaw, but he forced himself to move. Fast. Even though he wasn't sure what had just happened, he did know one thing for certain.

Someone had just tried to kill Delaney and him.

Cash managed to get to his feet, and he whirled around to check on Delaney. His heart rocketed to his knees when he saw the huge chunk of her home's burning roof on top of his truck. It had caved in the metal, and the flames were whipping through what was left of the windshield. Which wasn't much. But that wasn't the worst of it.

The worst was that Delaney was still inside the truck.

Behind him, there were shouts from the cops who'd just arrived on scene. One of them yelled for Cash to get back. He didn't listen. No way would he leave Delaney in there to be burned alive.

Obviously, Delaney didn't have plans for that, either, because she shoved open the passenger's-side door and practically spilled out into his arms. Cash caught her, pulling her away from the flames, and it was barely in the nick of time. Because the rest of the front windshield caved in, sending a wall of fire and glass right onto the seat where Delaney had just been sitting.

Beating out the embers that were smoking and sparking on her clothes, Cash dragged her away from the truck and into the center of the yard. He glanced up and got his first look at the house.

Hell.

The front of the structure was gone, obviously blown out by some kind of bomb. The rest of the place hadn't fared much better. What was left of the roof was groaning and creaking—ready to collapse—and the thick flames were eating their way from the floor to the ceiling.

"He blew up my house," Delaney muttered.

Cash was reasonably sure that she was in shock, but he didn't know if she'd been physically hurt as well. There were some small cuts and a bruise on her face, and he hoped that was the worst of it. However, she could have internal injuries. There was no telling what may have hit her when the building exploded.

"We have to move," Cash told her. The wind was sending the thick black smoke right at them, and Delaney was already starting to cough. They had enough to worry about without dealing with smoke inhalation.

"Get away from there!" someone yelled. Maybe one of the cops, and it was highly likely the shout was meant for them.

Cash hauled Delaney to her feet and pulled her against him, sheltering her from the heat of the fire, while he forced her to turn and start toward the cops. Cash could see them now, two of them, and they were frantically motioning for Delaney and him to move.

And Cash soon learned why.

Behind them, what remained of the fiery roof came crashing down, and it spewed smoke, flames and debris right at them. Cash could feel the scalding heat and knew it could hurt them both, so he scooped up Delaney and started running.

"I'm Cash Mercer, sheriff of Clay Ridge," he called out when he saw the alarm on the cops' faces. Alarm in part because Cash still had hold of his gun.

The two cops certainly didn't relax, but they hurried toward them to help Cash get Delaney away from the house.

"You're Delaney Archer?" one of the cops asked her. He was tall and lanky, in his early thirties, and had thinning brown hair. According to his name tag, he was N. Jenkins.

Coughing, she nodded, and Cash put her on the back seat of the cruiser when the second cop opened the door. This one, P. Chavez, was Hispanic and built like a heavyweight boxer.

Along with giving both Delaney and Cash some once-overs, Chavez and Jenkins continued to keep an eye on the fire. It wasn't spreading, but there was still a chance of that, especially if the winds picked up.

"What happened here?" Chavez asked, and he directed that particular question at Cash.

"Webb Bennison," Delaney answered before Cash could say anything. "He did this. He's done a lot of bad things."

Chavez and Jenkins exchanged a look that made Cash want to curse. Because Cash could see the skepticism flash in their eyes. Word had likely gotten out that the FBI thought Webb was dead, but the message on the wall of the foyer was proof that he was very much alive.

Except there was no longer a foyer wall. Which meant there was no longer any proof.

Cash wanted to kick himself for not getting a photo of what their attacker had written. That way, the lab could have examined it to see if there was anything that he'd missed, but his priority had been getting Delaney out of there. Good thing, too, because if they'd stayed inside, they would have been killed in the explosion.

"Someone left Delaney a message, a threat," Cash emphasized, "painted on the wall of the foyer.

It said, *'Delaney, there's no place for you to hide. Sooner or later, I will get to you.'*"

The cops exchanged another glance. "You saw this threat?" Chavez asked him.

"I did," Cash verified.

"And why are you here with Ms. Archer?" Chavez pressed after a short pause.

Cash had no intention of telling them that a dazed and out-of-it Delaney had shown up at his house the night before, but if they ran a background check on him, which they would certainly do, they'd learn the connection. Best to hear it from him so Chavez and Jenkins didn't think he was hiding something.

"Delaney and I were once engaged," Cash explained. "She came to me for help because Webb Bennison has been threatening her."

Cash heard the wail of the sirens, lots of them. Fire department, more cops, maybe even an ambulance. Soon, the place would be overrun by the first responders who would all be trying to do their jobs. Jobs that might not include pinning all of this on a man they believed to be dead.

Dragging in a long breath, Chavez shifted his attention to Delaney. "Ma'am, you've seen Webb? You know for certain that he's the one who did this?" He tipped his head to the fire.

Delaney took a long breath as well. "I didn't see Webb, but I know he's the one doing this." Her voice cracked, and Cash could see that she was trying to steel herself up. "He could have killed us."

"And Webb has a reason to murder Sheriff Mercer?" Jenkins asked.

"No," she answered, but then Delaney shook her head. "Maybe Webb wants Cash dead because of his connection to me."

Judging from the questions the cops were asking, they already knew about Delaney defending Webb. And that probably took her down a notch or two in their eyes. Everyone might deserve to have a lawyer, but cops didn't always have a lot of respect for those who defended criminals. That didn't mean they wouldn't do their jobs and investigate this. But Cash would do his own investigation. He had to find Webb and put him back behind bars before he could get to Delaney again.

When the ambulance pulled up in front of the house, Jenkins motioned for it to come closer. "The EMTs are going to take you both to the hospital to be checked out," he told Cash and Delaney.

"No," Delaney insisted. "I'm fine."

Cash figured her most recent hospital stay under psychiatric observation was playing into her quick response. He understood it, but he wanted Delaney checked to make sure she truly was okay.

"I should see a doctor," Cash said, rotating his shoulder as if it were hurting. It was. Actually, his chest and jaw were aching, too. Not enough for him to be carted to the hospital, but if he went, Delaney would come with him.

She stood, and there was alarm in her eyes. In

fact, she no longer looked in shock. Just concerned, and that concern was all for him. Cash felt a little guilty about playing that particular card, but along with the ploy causing Delaney to get an exam, it would also get her the heck away from what was left of her house. She didn't need to be here, to see the proof of what Webb had just tried to do to her.

Except maybe it wasn't Webb.

As a cop, he had to look at all angles, and it was possible someone else had done this to make it look as if Webb were responsible. Ramone, for instance. If Webb was truly dead, then maybe Ramone was doing some extreme gaslighting to get back at Delaney for not keeping his brother out of prison. But there was another possibility here, too.

The private investigator, Byers.

With all the calls, visits and tattling Byers was doing, it seemed to Cash that the PI was obsessed with Delaney. Maybe that obsession had taken an even darker turn that had led to an attempt on her life. Byers could have ditched his insistence that there was no threat to Delaney because it wasn't getting him what he possibly wanted—access to her. Then Byers could create the threat himself.

Yeah, that was definitely something Cash needed to check out.

As the fire department moved in to try to contain the flames, Cash led Delaney toward the ambulance. He holstered his gun, but he kept watch because the person who'd set that bomb could still be around. Watching. Waiting for another chance to kill them. But Cash didn't see anyone who set off his cop alarms.

But there was one person who had today. And that had been Gil. Cash didn't want to think the worst of Delaney's father, but it was hard not to do just that. Along with spending time in jail, Gil had also been in and out of mental institutions, and while Cash didn't see the man doing anything to hurt his daughter, there was the potential for Gil to go off the deep end and do something to try to hurt Jeb Mercer's son.

Hell.

He hoped that wasn't the case, that he'd just been put off by the man's venom over the bad blood with Jeb. But it was yet something else Cash needed to check off the list. If Gil had sent the text that'd gotten delayed, he could have done that, believing that Cash wouldn't take Delaney to her house until he was sure it was safe. He didn't know if Gil had any kind of explosives training or knowledge, but that went on Cash's to-do list as well.

The EMTs helped them into the ambulance, and when one of them put Delaney on the gurney, Cash took the seat next to her.

"What is it?" Delaney asked.

She reached out and touched Cash's hand, and that was when he realized she'd likely been staring at him while he was lost in thought. Thoughts about her father blowing her house, and maybe Cash himself, to smithereens.

Cash didn't plan to spell that out to her now. Not when she was still trembling from nearly being killed. It would only put a wedge between them because she'd feel the need to defend her father. Right now was a really bad time for wedges.

"I don't want you to give me a hassle about staying with me," he said. "I want you in my protective custody."

Even with everything that had just happened, Cash could see that she did indeed want to give him that hassle. Not because she didn't know the depths of the danger. No, she knew that all right. This was about her trying to keep him safe. Which was a load of crap. He was a cop, and this was his job.

Or rather Cash was making it his job.

A hired guard or the local cops didn't have the emotional investment he did. Of course, it was an *investment* he shouldn't have. But hey, it was there all right. Always there. And Cash just wasn't going to fight it when he knew he'd do everything to keep Delaney safe.

She might have seen that resolve in his eyes, because she finally nodded, and her grip tightened on his hand. "If you get yourself hurt protecting me, I'm going to be really mad at you."

Cash smiled. "Ditto," he said, and then he did something stupid.

He brushed his mouth over hers.

Talk about a wedge. Delaney went stiff, pulling her hand from his, and she got a panicked look in her eyes. A look Cash totally understood. They shouldn't be kissing. They shouldn't be doing anything to give in to this relentless heat that not even an explosion and near death could cool down.

Thankfully, they both got a quick distraction when the EMT's phone rang, the sound shooting through the back of the ambulance. But only a few seconds later, Cash was rethinking the *thankfully* part. The EMT looked plenty unsteady when he handed his phone to Cash.

"It's Jenkins," the EMT relayed, "the cop who responded to Ms. Archer's house. He wants to talk to you."

Cash didn't ask if the cop had told the EMT why he'd called. He just took the phone and hoped they weren't about to get another dose of bad news. However, the feeling in his gut told him to brace for the worst.

"Sheriff Mercer," Cash answered.

"I figured I'd give you the news and you could pass it along," Jenkins explained. "We just got a report about Ms. Archer's assistant, Melanie Adams. She's been kidnapped."

Cash felt the initial slam of adrenaline, but he tried to keep his expression neutral so that Delaney wouldn't panic. "Do you have any details of how it happened or who took her?" he snapped.

"According to an eyewitness, a man wearing a

ski mask dragged her out of the office at gunpoint and forced her into a truck."

Cash silently cursed. Because he could see it all playing out. And he knew Melanie had to be terrified.

"The eyewitness didn't get the license plate or a description of the truck, for that matter," Jenkins continued, and then he paused. "But according to the message left inside the office, the man who took her was Webb Bennison."

"What message?" Cash demanded.

"I'm sending a photo of it now," Jenkins assured him.

Cash avoided eye contact with Delaney while he waited for the dinging sound to indicate the photo had loaded. Like the message left in Delaney's foyer, this one was also written in red paint with the words scrawled across six or more feet on the wall.

Words that would tear Delaney to pieces.

Chapter Seven

This is your fault, Delaney. I took Melanie because of you. Love, Webb.

Even though Delaney had barely gotten a look at the picture that Officer Jenkins had sent Cash, a glimpse was all she needed for the message to be burned into her mind.

A message that was true.

It was her fault that Webb had kidnapped Melanie. She'd been so caught up in dealing with the aftermath of her escape from the hospital that she hadn't warned Melanie. Something she should have done right after the dizziness and the disorientation had worn off. It didn't matter that it was what Delaney had planned to do. No. That didn't matter at all.

The bottom line was that she hadn't acted fast enough, and because she hadn't, Melanie was now in the hands of a killer.

"You should keep watch," Cash said, pulling Delaney out of her thoughts. Something he'd been doing a lot since they'd left Lubbock and started the drive to his ranch in the truck he'd rented.

Delaney was keeping watch. Making sure they weren't being followed. Checking to see if they were about to be ambushed on the country road. But with the weariness scraping her raw all the way to the bone, it probably looked to Cash as if she were about to zone out on him. Part of her wanted to do that, to escape so that she didn't have to feel this fear she had for Melanie. But the fear wasn't the only thing she was feeling. There was plenty of anger, too. Anger at herself and especially at Webb for taking his vendetta out on an innocent woman who'd only been doing her job.

It'd been nearly eight hours since Delaney had seen a picture of that message Webb had left at her office. The ambulance had taken them to the hospital, where she and Cash had gotten their minor burns and cuts treated. After that, two cops had driven them to the police station to give their statements.

Delaney had put herself on autopilot to go over all the details that the cops had wanted. Just getting it done, going over all the things about Webb that she wished were only part of her past and not playing into what was happening now.

Because Webb was indeed part of what was *happening now*, Delaney had also used Cash's phone so she could make some security arrangements. She'd hired a PI/bodyguard to go to her father's house to stay with him. Gil hadn't appreciated the guard and had told her so when she'd called him. However, since she had also filled him in on the explosion, he knew there was the possibility of danger spilling over onto him.

"You think it's a mistake for me not to be with my father?" she asked, knowing it would cause that flash of worry in Cash's eyes.

It did. Maybe because he knew Gil wouldn't welcome him into his house even if it meant she'd be safer with Cash around. But as Delaney studied Cash, she thought there might be something more.

"Other than the obvious, what exactly are you worried about?" she added to her question. "Do you think my father wouldn't put my safety above his hatred for you?"

"Maybe," Cash answered after a very long hesitation. "Not purposely, though. I don't think he'd intentionally put you at risk." He paused again, studied her. "Do you?"

Delaney opened her mouth to give him a quick no, but she didn't think she was mistaking Cash's tone. *He* thought it was possible that Gil could hurt her.

Even though Delaney didn't especially want her thoughts to go in that direction, she played around with some possible scenarios that could have caused Cash to ask that particular question.

"You believe that if my father starts drinking it might lead him to do something dangerous?" she suggested. "Like try to lure Webb out to stop him from coming after me?"

And just her saying that aloud made her realize it was true. Oh, mercy. It was true.

Her father had a temper, a really bad one that stayed contained most of the time. But if he unleashed it with the help of some alcohol, he could want a showdown with Webb. One that Gil would lose. Webb was a lot younger and lot stronger. Not to mention a lot more desperate.

"I need to use your phone," she insisted.

Cash pulled it from his pocket and handed it to her. "You're calling your father?"

"No, the PI I hired."

No need to clarify that she hadn't meant Byers. She'd learned her lesson with him and had gone with a large agency, one with a sterling reputation, and they had assigned Trevor Salvetti, who also had bodyguard training. Salvetti had gone straight to her father's house and now answered her call on the first ring.

"This is Delaney Archer," she said. "I need you to make sure my father doesn't get out of your sight. He might try to leave and contact Webb Bennison."

"He hasn't tried that so far," Salvetti assured her. "But I'll definitely keep my eye on him. FYI, he's not happy about me being here."

"No," she agreed. Delaney had known that would be his reaction, but she could deal with his anger as long as he was safe. "Uh, he hasn't had anything to drink, has he? I mean alcohol." She mentally cringed because this was definitely going behind her father's back, but she had to be sure the situation hadn't sent him back over the edge.

"If he has, I haven't seen any signs of it," the PI answered, "but I'll keep my eye out for it."

Thankfully, Salvetti didn't press her on the details of why she'd asked the question in the first place. Good thing because Delaney didn't want to spell out that her father was a mean drunk who often made bad decisions.

"Any word on your missing assistant?" Salvetti wanted to know. Delaney had filled him in on that when she'd hired him.

"No. Not yet." But Delaney held on to the hope that Webb would be contacting her soon with some kind of ransom demand.

Not money.

No, that wasn't what Webb wanted. He wanted her, and Delaney suspected Webb would demand a trade—her for Melanie. That would be their best-case scenario unless the cops managed to find Melanie soon. It was entirely possible that Webb would just murder Melanie to make Delaney suffer. And it would. It would cut deep.

She ended the call with the PI and handed Cash back his phone. Delaney avoided eye contact with him because she didn't want him to see that she was barely holding on by a thread. But he must have sensed it anyway.

"I know you're worried about Webb possibly going after your father or vice versa," Cash said. "But I get the feeling there's something more. Something about Gil that you're not telling me."

Delaney wanted to curse. Cash was a good cop, but she hadn't wanted him to pick up on the nerves simmering beneath the obvious. Because, yes, there was plenty about her father that she hadn't told him.

She kept her gaze on the road as Cash made the turn off the interstate and took the exit for Clay Ridge. "My father doesn't always think straight when he's been drinking."

Cash made a quick sound of agreement. "Got that. And you're concerned the not thinking straight could cause him to take a risk with Webb. Got that, too, but there's more to it than that," he quickly added. "What's going on with your father?"

She could read the subtext. Cash wanted to know why she continued to keep close ties with her father when it was obvious their relationship was strained and at times even toxic.

"He defended you," Cash continued when she didn't say anything. "You blame yourself because he went to jail—"

"It was all my fault," she blurted out before he could start laying out the reasons why she shouldn't feel guilty. "I knew Aaron Skyler was bad, and I took him to the house anyway."

"You sure as hell didn't take him there so he could rape you," Cash snarled.

"No," she quietly agreed.

But she'd known Aaron would likely want to make out with her, and she'd wanted the same. At least she had until he'd started to push her for more and she'd said no. Aaron hadn't accepted her "no," and had started tearing away at her clothes. Aaron had done that after he'd punched her in the face. By the time her father had come in, she was bruised, bleeding and terrified.

"And you didn't ask your father to kill Aaron," Cash added. He'd softened his voice as well.

"No," she repeated. "But he did kill him and then went to jail for it."

Cash huffed, then sighed. "And just like he said—seeing me is a reminder of what happened. I can curse my DNA for the umpteenth time. I know I'm the spitting image of how Jeb looked when he was in his thirties. I bring back the bad memories for your father. You know that, and that's why you try to shelter him from me. That's what tore us apart, and it'll keep on tearing—"

"My father tried to kill himself," she blurted out.

Judging from the shock she saw on Cash's face, this was one bit of info that he hadn't heard. Then again, Delaney had worked hard to keep it under wraps because she'd known Gil wouldn't be able to face the pity or the looks that he was a broken man.

"I never heard anything about this," Cash muttered.

Delaney nodded. Sighed. She hadn't intended

to tell him, not like this anyway, but maybe it was time for him to know. But she had to take a deep breath before she continued.

"He tried twice," she explained. "Booze and sleeping pills both times. The second time was worse than the first, and he barely survived. That's when he told me he'd rather be dead than have to see me with you."

Cash groaned and then cursed. "When did he tell you that? When the hell did this happen?"

Again, she needed a deep breath. "Right before I ended our engagement." And that was all she had to say for Cash to fill in a lot of blanks.

Yes, her father was the reason she'd broken up with him. Yes, she'd been terrified of a third suicide attempt, one that would end his life. Or worse.

"I was the one who found my father after both attempts," she continued. "With the second one, he was groggy, and mumbling. Maybe talking out of his head. But he mentioned that it might be better off if we were both dead. You and me," Delaney clarified, pointing to Cash. "Later, I asked him about it, and he said he didn't remember. But I think that when he's been drinking he sometimes wishes you and I weren't around. After all, I'm also a reminder of the night he killed a boy, and you're a reminder of Jeb and his arrest."

Cash stayed quiet for several long moments before he cursed. "You should have told me this," he snapped.

As expected, there was plenty of anger in his voice. With reason. Cash now knew that she'd broken off their engagement to save her father.

Maybe to save Cash, too.

Delaney didn't want to believe that her father would go to such a dark place that he'd try to kill Cash, or her, and then end his own life, but believing Gil wouldn't have hurt or killed Cash had seemed a huge risk to take. Of course, if she'd told Cash, he would have tried to help her work it out. She had loved Cash too much to put that on him.

When Cash cursed again, she thought that maybe he was about to verbally blast her for holding back about Gil's suicide attempts. But when she looked up, Delaney realized the cursing wasn't for her or their situation. It was because there were two vehicles parked in front of his house. There were also two men standing by those vehicles, and while Delaney didn't recognize one, she did the other.

"That's Kevin Byers," she snapped.

It was now her turn to curse. She hadn't had time to go by his office and tell the PI to back the heck off, but she could certainly do that now. Just seeing him here at Cash's ranch washed away some of the bone-weary fatigue caused by the adrenaline crash, and Delaney likely would have bolted from the truck when it came to a stop if Cash hadn't taken hold of her arm.

"And who's the second man?" Cash asked.

She shook her head, glared at Byers through the windshield. "I've never seen him before."

He was short and beefy with a wrestler's build, and he was wearing a dark gray suit with the jacket unbuttoned. He turned, causing the light to glint off the badge clipped to his belt. The badge she recognized.

It belonged to an FBI agent.

Delaney felt her stomach tighten. *What now?* The day had already been plenty bad enough, and she prayed the agent wasn't there to give her bad news about Melanie.

Byers and the man with the badge weren't the only ones in Cash's front yard. Two of his ranch hands were there, too, and both were armed. They were obviously keeping watch, and the hands moved toward them when Cash and she got out of the truck. One of them was Stoney Quates, who'd worked for Cash for years, and judging by the strong resemblance, the younger man was his son.

"They insisted on waiting for you," Stoney told Cash, and the hand obviously wasn't pleased about that. Probably because the ranch was basically on lockdown right now.

"I'm Special Agent Van Curley," the FBI agent volunteered, his voice no-nonsense and all lawman. He spared Cash a glance before nailing his attention to Delaney. "Ms. Archer?" He didn't continue until she gave an acknowledging nod. "You and I need to talk."

"I need to talk to you, too," Byers insisted. As usual, the man reeked of the aftershave he obviously favored, and the scent only made Delaney's stomach even more unsettled. "Now," he added like an order that he was dead certain she would obey.

Delaney didn't roll her eyes. Instead, she narrowed them. "We have nothing to discuss," she warned Byers. "In fact, I don't want you here, and I don't want you contacting people about me. My business with you is finished. If you don't stop hounding me, I'll file a restraining order."

That caused Byers's own eyes to narrow. "You're conning people to make them believe you're in danger. You're not. You're making false claims that are tying up the law enforcement officers who need to be concentrating on finding Webb Bennison's body so they can put this all to rest."

Cash riled her when he stepped in front of her. Delaney wanted to blister Byers with a glare and a response, and she didn't need help for that. Still, Cash obviously felt the need to do the same.

"Delaney was nearly killed when someone blew up her house. Then someone kidnapped her assistant. Webb Bennison, probably. Delaney *is* in danger, period, and you're not welcome here. Leave or I'll arrest you for trespassing."

Byers didn't budge. "It's Delaney's DNA on the envelope of the so-called threatening letter she got from Webb," the PI snarled. "Go ahead. Ask Special Agent Curley here. He'll tell you the same."

Curley sighed, nodded. "The lab reran the test. It's her DNA, all right."

"And someone could have set her up," Cash pointed out. "It's not that hard to get someone's DNA. From her trash. From a water glass she used at a restaurant." Cash shifted his attention back to Byers. "In fact, you could have done that because she fired you."

She could practically see the temper bubbling up in Byers, but then he seemed to rein in the anger. "I could have done that," the PI admitted, "but I didn't." He groaned and squeezed his eyes shut for a moment. "I just need all of this to go away. I need to put it behind me."

That was a lot of emotion for a mere case that he'd no longer been hired to do. "What are you talking about?" Delaney demanded.

But Byers shook his head, waved her off and hurried toward his vehicle.

"You know him well?" Curley asked, his attention on Byers as he sped off.

"No," Delaney answered. "I hired him to find Webb, and then I fired him."

Curley's forehead bunched up. "Did Byers develop feelings for you?" Curley pressed, but then he waved that off. "Sorry, the hazards of the job. It just seems to me that you two might be together." He motioned to Cash and her. "And I was thinking Byers might be jealous. The kind of jealousy that sends someone into a rant like we just witnessed."

Cash made a quick sound of agreement and drew in a long breath. He didn't shift his attention off Byers until the PI's vehicle was no longer in sight. "Why don't we take this chat inside?" Cash asked, but he didn't wait for Curley to agree. He took hold of Delaney's hand and led her to the front door. "I don't want Delaney standing around outside to give someone the chance to attack her again."

Curley made his own sound of agreement, and the three of them went in when Stoney opened the door for them.

"Nobody else has been here today?" Cash asked the ranch hand.

"Nobody," Stoney confirmed. "You want me to wait in here with you until your *company* leaves?" He cast an uneasy glance at Curley.

"No, it's okay. I want you on the porch in case Byers comes back."

Stoney muttered, "Will do," and he headed back out to the porch.

Delaney didn't waste any time getting her point across to the agent. "If you're here to arrest me for making a false report, then you're making a huge mistake. I didn't send myself that threatening note, and I didn't blow up my house or kidnap my assistant."

"I believe you," Curley said without even a second of hesitation.

She had to do a mental double take and bite off the rest of the argument she'd been prepared to deliver. "You believe me," Delaney repeated, her voice thick with relief. But there was also some skepticism.

She wasn't anywhere close to being steady right now, but it was possible the agent was placating her to get on her good side. Perhaps because he thought it would encourage her to confess to any wrongdoing.

"Yes," the agent verified. "Webb's a killer, and if he's alive, I could see him going after you like this."

"If he's alive," she repeated, and some of the frustration returned. "You think he's dead?"

"I think he *could be* dead," Curley corrected. "His brother could be behind the attacks and threats."

"Especially since Ramone is now my new neighbor," Cash tossed out there. "Along with his business partner, he bought the ranch next to mine."

Curley's eyes widened with surprise. Obviously, he hadn't gotten the word about that yet. "You're sure?"

"Dead sure. Ramone paid Delaney and me a visit this morning. He played nice. Well, nice enough," Cash amended, "considering he has dogs that have probably been trained to attack. Dogs that got loose and came onto my property, where they could have hurt Delaney."

Curley took a moment, clearly processing that, and grumbled some profanity. "The FBI has been keeping tabs on Ramone since his brother's escape.

Obviously, though, we haven't been careful enough if we missed something like that. You believe Ramone is here to taunt Delaney?"

"Or try to finish her off for Webb," Cash said, but then he was the one to mutter a curse. "Sorry," he added to Delaney.

It had spiked her heart rate a couple of notches to hear Cash spell it out like that, but Delaney had already come to that same conclusion. Ramone might be the sole threat, the person responsible for all the horrible things that had been going on. Maybe he was doing that because his brother was indeed dead, and Ramone had taken it upon himself to exact revenge.

"I had a deputy put up security cameras on the property line I share with Ramone," Cash continued a moment later. "The deputy's monitoring the feed so we'll know if Webb shows up."

"I'd like for you to share anything on that feed that could be connected to this investigation," Curley insisted. And it was indeed an insistence. "I can get a court order," he added when Cash paused.

"No need," Cash assured him, his stare boring into Curley. "I'll share, but if I get one whiff that you or anyone in your agency is coming after Delaney for false reports and such, my cooperation with you will end in a snap."

Judging from the flicker of annoyance in the agent's eyes, Curley didn't care much for that, but he didn't get a chance to voice his objection because Stoney called out to them.

"Boss, you got a visitor," the ranch hand announced, opening the door a fraction.

"Is it the PI?" Cash snapped.

"No. Uh, it's your dad."

Cash got the same surprised expression that Curley had when he'd found out about Ramone buying the adjacent ranch. Unless things had changed since she'd broken off their engagement, Jeb Mercer didn't make a habit of coming out to visit his son.

"Excuse me a minute," Cash muttered, and he tipped his head for Delaney to follow him to the door. Perhaps because he didn't want to leave her alone with Curley in case the agent started to interrogate her.

Cash opened the door wider, but he positioned himself so that he was standing in front of her. Still protecting her. Though she doubted Jeb would be a threat. Still, a sniper could fire into the doorway, and that was a reminder for her to keep watch. And to make this visit short if Cash wasn't planning on inviting Jeb inside.

From over Cash's shoulder, Delaney saw Jeb step from his truck. He looked a lot older than he had the last time she'd seen him, and from beneath his Stetson, she could see the sides of his hair were mostly gray. Still, he managed to look formidable, maybe because he'd taken on a bogeyman status because of what he had done to her own father.

"I'm here on business," Jeb said, probably noting the extreme disapproval in Cash's eyes.

Because she had her arm next to Cash's, she felt his muscles stay tight. "What kind of business?"

Jeb shifted his gaze to Delaney. "I thought you'd want to know. I found your assistant. I found Melanie."

Chapter Eight

"You found Melanie?" Delaney said, her breath rushing out with the words.

She might have rushed out to Jeb, too, if Cash hadn't held her back. Cash didn't want Webb or anyone else to get an easy shot at Delaney, and her going out into the open would definitely make it easier.

"Where? How?" Cash asked Jeb, and he also wanted to know how his father had gotten involved in this. Jeb was no longer the sheriff and lived miles from Lubbock, where Melanie had been kidnapped.

"I got an anonymous call," Jeb explained as he walked to the porch. He made a sweeping glance around the yard. The kind of glance a cop would make. "The caller said a missing woman, Melanie Adams, was at the end of my road. I went down there and found her. She was tied up and gagged."

"She's alive?" Delaney blurted out. Her breath was gusting now, and Cash could practically feel the hope coming off her in waves.

Jeb nodded. "She has some cuts and bruises. A broken finger, too. I got her to the hospital and had the security guard stay with her. I considered calling you but figured I'd better drive out and give you the news in person."

Cash mentally went through everything Jeb had just told them, and he got hit with a whole mountain of concerns. Not only was he troubled by what Leigh had said about Jeb's health problem, Cash was also concerned that the anonymous call could have been a hoax to lure Jeb out so he could be taken and then used to "negotiate" with Delaney and him.

Or Jeb could have been gunned down.

Webb or whoever was behind the attacks might not realize that Jeb and he didn't exactly have a loving relationship and could have planned Jeb's murder as a way to punish Cash for helping Delaney. Thankfully, none of that had happened.

Cash's next round of questions and concerns dealt with the big picture. A puzzling big picture. Why the heck had Melanie's kidnapper left her by Jeb's ranch? And why hadn't the kidnapper just killed her? Cash had figured the point in taking the woman was to use her as a sort of ransom to get to Delaney. But maybe this had been just another taunt. If so, Cash would take it. Delaney, too. Because a taunt was a hell of a lot better than Delaney's assistant being dead.

"I need to get to the hospital," Delaney insisted. "I have to see Melanie."

Cash had known she was going to want to do that. He would have wanted the same thing in her place. But the problem was getting Delaney safely to and from Dark River. Maybe that had been the point of Melanie's abduction—to get Delaney into a position where she could be attacked, killed or taken.

None of those possibilities were acceptable.

"I can follow you to the hospital," Jeb offered.

"So can I," Agent Curley spoke up. He'd obviously heard the conversation.

Cash didn't bother with introductions. He focused on the best way to go from here to there, and having two backups might not guarantee Delaney's safety, but it would get her there faster because he wouldn't have to wait for one of his deputies to arrive.

"Thanks," Cash told both Jeb and Curley, and he turned back to Jeb. "Was Melanie able to tell you anything about her kidnapping?"

Jeb shook his head. "She was pretty shaken up. In shock, you know."

Cash had figured that was the case, and he knew that Delaney was shaken up as well. "Give me a minute with Delaney," Cash said, speaking to both Jeb and the agent.

Curley nodded. "I'll wait in my car." He stepped around them to go outside and toward his vehicle.

When Jeb headed back to his truck, Cash closed the door so he could lay out some ground rules for Delaney and try to steel her up for what could turn out to be a gut-wrenching visit with Melanie. However, he didn't even get a chance to start because Delaney went straight into his arms. The sound she made was part sob, part relief.

"Melanie's alive," she whispered, her voice hoarse and clogged with everything she was feeling.

Cash sighed and brushed a kiss on the top of her head. He hated to remind her of this, but it had to be done. "Going to see her could be a trap."

"I know. But Melanie's alive."

Yeah, that was definitely a good bottom line. Added to that, Melanie might be able to give him details about who'd taken her. She might be able to ID Webb as her kidnapper. If so, that would convince any naysayers who were still clinging to the notion that Webb was dead.

As if she'd just remembered something, Delaney's head whipped up from his shoulder. "Webb could go after her again."

Cash could give her some reassurance on this. "Jeb said the security guard's with her, and I'll text Leigh to have her assign a protection detail." Something that his sister had already likely done since Leigh was a damn good cop.

"We can't let Webb hurt her again." There was a frantic edge to Delaney's voice now, and he saw that edge mirrored in her eyes. She'd been through the wringer over the past couple of days, and something like this—even though it was good news about Melanie being alive—could break her.

"We won't," he assured her. "Melanie will be guarded, and when she's released from the hospital, she'll be moved to a safe house."

While she blinked back tears, Delaney searched his face as if she was trying to make sure he was telling her the truth. He was. But what he was holding back was that Melanie might already be broken. Some people just couldn't come back from a trauma like this, and Cash was betting that her captor hadn't made any part of this ordeal easy for her.

"We'll get Melanie the help she needs," Cash settled for saying.

Delaney continued to stare at him for several moments, and then she finally released the breath she'd been holding.

And then she kissed him.

Cash sure hadn't seen that coming, but her mouth landed on his, giving him a quick hit of her taste and the heat. Oh, yeah. This was a hit all right, and she didn't stop with just a celebratory peck. This was a full-fledged kiss, long and deep. The kind of kiss they'd usually shared right before they'd landed in bed.

He felt the heat slide through him. Felt his body start to nudge him to take the kiss and run with it. Straight to the bed. But the timing sucked. And that was why Cash forced himself to ease away from her.

Blinking, Delaney looked up at him, her breath gusting against his mouth. She looked like a woman coming out of a dream. A hot woman. One he wanted way too much.

"We should go," Cash said, not only as a reminder to her but also for himself.

She nodded but didn't move. Delaney kept her gaze fixed on him. "I'll never forget what you've done for me. For Melanie," she added.

And that was the perfect thing for her to say to slap him out of his own dream state. Delaney was grateful, and that was the reason she'd kissed him. Well, the heat had probably played into it for her, too, but it was gratitude that had started this particular ball rolling, and that gave Cash another reminder. She'd broken up with him for a reason.

Because of her father.

That reason was still there. Delaney wouldn't be able to live with herself if being with him again caused Gil to take his own life. That meant the kisses and the heat were just a torment right now. One that could complicate things when more than ever he needed a clear head.

"Let's go," he said, drawing his gun.

Cash stepped out onto the porch and glanced around before he led Delaney to the rental truck. As he'd done with their previous trip, he had her sink lower in the seat so she wouldn't be an easy target, and he pulled out of his driveway with both Jeb and Curley following them. Maybe, just maybe, having the close proximity of the other vehicles would discourage someone from attacking.

While he kept watch, Cash used the hands-free function to send a text to Leigh, asking her about the protection detail. As expected, he got a quick response with just one word. Done.

Good. That was one thing off his plate, so he then called Jesse to get his deputy started on a few things.

"You're okay?" Jesse immediately asked.

Cash understood his deputy's edgy tone. Jesse had it for a good reason since he knew all about what had gone on at Delaney's house.

"You're on speaker," Cash informed Jesse. "And Delaney's right here with me."

Of course, that meant Cash wanted Jesse to be mindful of the way he responded, but it caused Delaney to huff. Obviously, she didn't want "mindful," but she was getting it anyway.

"Delaney's assistant is alive and in the Dark River Hospital," Cash explained to Jesse. "Delaney and I are on the way to see her now."

Again, Jesse was quick with the question. "You need backup?"

"No, I have it." And Cash made an uneasy glance in the rearview mirror.

He wasn't exactly comfortable being around Jeb or an FBI agent who might or might not believe

Delaney had created a hoax threat. But if it came down to it, Cash figured both men were capable of helping him fight off Webb.

"The FBI wants a look at any suspicious feed from the security cameras," Cash explained. "I'm guessing there hasn't been any or you would have called me."

"I would have," Jesse assured him. "Other than a few ranch hands and the dogs, no one appeared on the camera, but the house is big, and if Ramone knew we were filming him, he could have sneaked out back."

Cash had already come to that same conclusion. There was a barn not far from the house, and Ramone could have slipped in there and left out the back to get to one of the old ranch trails that threaded through the property. From there, he could have had a vehicle waiting for him. A vehicle that he could have used to get to Delaney's, where he left the message and set the explosion.

"Is there anything in Ramone's background about him having experience with building bombs?" Cash asked.

"Nothing, but that doesn't mean he didn't learn that particular skill."

No, it didn't. Which meant Cash wouldn't be taking Ramone off his suspect list anytime soon.

"I did find out something else," Jesse continued a moment later. "Something on that PI you asked me to run a check on."

"Kevin Byers," Cash supplied. He had indeed asked Jesse for a check, but Cash also intended to do some digging of his own. "What'd you find?"

"Well, it's nothing criminal, but it's definitely interesting. Did you know Byers has a connection to Webb? A *personal* connection," Jesse emphasized.

That got Delaney's attention. "Personal? How?" she demanded, taking the questions right out of Cash's mouth.

"This didn't come out in Webb's trial," Jesse explained, "but I found Byers mentioned a couple of times on social media pages that belonged to a friend of Beatrice Stockwell."

Cash instantly recognized the name. She'd been Webb's girlfriend, and Webb had been convicted of killing her during a heated argument.

"This friend, Sasha Mondale, also posted pictures of her together with Beatrice and Byers." Jessie paused. "I contacted Sasha, and she claims Beatrice and Byers were having an affair right around the time Beatrice was killed."

Delaney shook her head. "Webb never mentioned this. Did he know?"

"According to Sasha, he did," Jesse answered.

Delaney huffed. "Why didn't Sasha report that to the cops? It would have gone to motive for Webb killing Beatrice."

"Because Sasha doesn't trust cops. And because Sasha said she was too scared to tell."

"Scared of Webb?" Cash pressed.

"No." Jesse paused a heartbeat. "Of Byers. In fact, Sasha doesn't believe Webb's guilty. She believes Byers is the one who murdered Beatrice."

"BYERS," DELANEY REPEATED.

She got a sick feeling in the pit of her stomach. Sick because this was a man she'd been stupid enough to hire. But was he a man who could have also killed? Delaney wasn't so sure of that. She'd seen his temper, and he was a bully, but he'd never been physical with her.

"Webb never confessed to killing Beatrice," Cash muttered. "Did he ever admit it to you?" he asked, and Delaney knew the question was meant for her.

"No. Not an actual confession, but there was a smugness to his denial." And that smugness had carried over into what he'd anticipated the outcome of his trial would be.

Webb had believed with 100 percent certainty that he would be found innocent.

When that hadn't happened, he was enraged, and Delaney had thought she'd seen the true colors of a killer. Unlike Byers, Webb had pushed her and even tried to take a swing at her before the bailiff had restrained him. Webb had shown he could be violent.

But what if he hadn't murdered Beatrice?

That would also account for the rage. Webb could have blamed that miscarriage of justice on her. So it was possible that Webb had been innocent. Of murder, anyway.

"I'll need to talk to Sasha," Delaney insisted.

"I thought you might want to," Jesse said. "I'll text Cash her contact info right now." Seconds later, Cash's phone dinged with the incoming message from Jesse. "Remember, though, that part about her not trusting cops. I'm pretty sure her mistrust extends to lawyers, too."

"Is Sasha credible?" Cash asked. "Is it possible she's got a reason for saying Byers murdered Beatrice?"

"Don't know. She doesn't have a police record, and she appears to be law-abiding. Still, she could have a grudge against Byers. Heck, maybe he was her ex-lover, and she wants to get back at him for having an affair with Beatrice."

That was possible, but Delaney still wanted to talk face-to-face with the woman. How she could make that happen, she didn't know. Cash would agree to a phone conversation, but it'd be a risk for her to meet with Sasha. Unless Delaney could talk the woman into meeting her at the police station. Cash might go along with that as long as he could be there with her.

Cash ended the call with his deputy, and for a few moments, he was quiet, but Delaney figured he was mentally trying to work all of this out. Just as she was trying to do.

He took the exit for Dark River, and Delaney saw the sign. Only five miles. Not far, but this was still a farm road with lots of places for an attacker to hide.

For Byers to hide.

"How and why did you hire Byers?" Cash finally asked.

Delaney wanted all of this out in the open, so she could try to make sense of it, but it still wasn't an easy subject for her. For one, it brought back memories of Webb. It also made her feel like a fool for ever allowing Byers into her life.

"I got the threatening letter," she explained. "And I was also positive someone was following me. So I called a few lawyer friends and asked them for recommendations for a PI. The cops were investigating the letter, but I wanted more. Someone to push hard to find out who'd sent it and who was following me. I figured a PI could do that, and yes, I know that sounds like a slap to the cops, but..." She stopped and lifted her shoulder.

"Cops don't always have time to follow through on threats, especially when there's been no escalation of violence," Cash finished for her.

She nodded before she continued. "I was in the process of narrowing down the list of PIs that I'd gotten when Byers came to my office. He rattled off the name of one of my friends and said he'd heard that I was looking for a PI."

"You didn't verify that with your friend or vet him?" Cash pressed.

Yes, she definitely felt like a fool. "No. I was really shaken up, and I just wanted quick answers. If Webb was following me, I wanted it to stop." She muttered a profanity. "You don't have to tell me how stupid I was—"

"Not stupid," Cash interrupted. "You weren't thinking straight." He dragged in a long breath. "And Byers might have taken advantage of that. Hell, he could have been the reason you weren't thinking straight to begin with, because maybe he was the one following you."

That put ice in her blood, and her stomach didn't just tighten. Everything inside her twisted and knotted. "You really think Byers could be the person trying to kill me?"

Cash stared at her. "What was it he said back at my house? *I just need all of this to go away. I need to put it behind me.*"

Yes, Byers had indeed said that, and it had confused her. Delaney had thought that maybe Byers had meant the bitterness over their failed working relationship, but maybe it was a whole lot more than that.

"You think Byers is feeling guilty because he might have gotten Beatrice killed?" she suggested.

Cash nodded. "If he didn't do the actual killing, Webb might have murdered her if he found out about the affair with Byers. Something like that could make a man obsessed with getting justice."

True, but Byers wasn't obsessed with Webb. The obsession seemed to be for her.

"But if Byers killed Beatrice," Delaney said, "then he could be enraged at me for not getting

Webb an acquittal. Maybe that only deepened Byers's feelings of guilt because Webb was behind bars and he wasn't."

However, that didn't explain why Byers would insist that Webb was dead. Or try to pin those threats on her. Again, it could be guilt, not wanting to deal with the fact that Webb might not be "dead" if he hadn't ended up in prison in the first place.

And that went straight back to Delaney.

She wanted to play around with that idea some more, but Delaney pushed it aside when Cash pulled into the parking lot of the Dark River Hospital. Curley and Jeb parked on each side of Cash's rental truck, and they all got out together. The three lawmen flanked her as they hurried inside.

"Melanie's in room 111," Jeb told them. He stayed back while they went to the room.

Delaney was relieved to see an armed deputy standing guard outside the door, and she would thank Leigh for that first chance she got. Obviously, the deputy recognized Cash because he stepped aside.

"I'd like to talk to her when you're done," Curley reminded them, and as Jeb had done, he stayed back in the hall when Cash and she went into the room.

Delaney saw Melanie in the hospital bed, and she felt another avalanche of emotions. Normally, there wasn't a strand of Melanie's long blond hair out of place, but right now it was a tangled mess.

And there was blood in it.

Delaney could also see the cuts and bruises. So many bruises. Melanie's face was covered with them, and her bottom lip was split. There was a splint on her right hand, no doubt to stabilize the broken finger.

"I'm okay," Melanie insisted, probably because she could see that Delaney was shaken to the core. "The doctor said my injuries are superficial."

The physical injuries probably were, but Delaney knew Melanie would be living with this nightmare for a long time. So would she.

Delaney went to her, maneuvering around the IV, so she could lean down and give Melanie a hug. She kept it light, barely making contact, because Delaney didn't want to add to the pain that Melanie was no doubt already feeling.

"I'm so sorry," Delaney whispered, and even though she fought the tears, they came anyway.

"This isn't your fault," Melanie muttered, and she was crying, too. And also shaking. Delaney could feel her trembling as she stroked Melanie's arm. "This is the fault of the man who took me."

The man. Not Webb. Delaney tried not to let her disappointment show when she pulled back from the hug, but she'd hoped—prayed even—that Melanie would be able to name Webb as her abductor.

Cash stepped closer. "Melanie, you remember me?" he asked.

Melanie nodded. "Cash Mercer. You're a cop, and your father's the one who found me."

Cash nodded, too, and eased even closer. "Yeah, and I want to make sure Delaney and you are safe." He kept his voice low and steady. None of the emotion that Delaney was feeling, but she was certain the emotion was there. Cash was just tamping it down to keep Melanie calm.

"Are we safe?" Melanie asked, her bottom lip quivering.

"You are," Cash assured her.

Delaney wanted to hang on to that, to believe it was true. And in Melanie's case, it probably was. After all, she was alive, and she could have been killed at any point during her captivity. The person who'd taken her hadn't done that, so it likely meant he wouldn't try to kill her again.

"My sister's the sheriff here in Dark River, and she's assigned deputies to protect you," Cash added, and then he paused. "I know this is hard, but anything you can tell me about your kidnapping might help. Do you know who took you?"

Melanie shook her head, a fast jerky motion as if she was trying to fight away the images of what had happened to her. "He came up from behind me. I guess he broke in through the backdoor or window in Delaney's office and then sneaked up on me. The front door was locked because we didn't have any appointments scheduled. I was there to catch up on some paperwork."

"You were at your desk?" Delaney asked, hoping to ease Melanie into the rest of the explanation.

It sickened her though to think that Webb or who-ever had done this had used her own office door to break in.

"Yes," Melanie confirmed. "I heard footsteps, but before I could turn around and look, it was too late. He bashed me on the head and knocked me out."

"But you're sure it was a man?" Cash pressed.

"Positive." Melanie stopped and took several shallow breaths. "When I came to, my hands were tied and I had on a blindfold, but he was carrying me so I could feel his chest muscles. It was a man," she added in a mutter.

Webb and Ramone were certainly strong enough to lift a woman and carry her to an escape vehicle. But so were plenty of men. In fact, Webb could have hired a thug to do the job for him.

"What else do you remember?" Cash asked.

"Not much. He kept me blindfolded, even when he was hitting me." Melanie cringed, fought for composure as she sat up. "He didn't use his fists. I think it was a leather sap or maybe a billy club. He just kept hitting me," she said, the words rushing out with a fresh round of tears.

Delaney gathered Melanie into her arms. "It's okay. You're safe now," she reminded her.

"I know," Melanie said on a sob. "And I know it's important that I tell you all of this, but I didn't see his face, and he never once spoke to me."

That last part was interesting. And perhaps telling. Maybe he hadn't spoken because Melanie would have recognized his voice. She almost certainly would have recognized Webb's, because Melanie had been in court every day when Webb was on trial. Ditto for Ramone's.

"I don't know where he took me," Melanie continued a moment later. "I think we stayed in the car or truck the whole time until he put me by the side of the road. I figured he was going to leave me to die because I was there for hours before Mr. Mercer came and rescued me."

"Hours," Delaney repeated, looking at Cash.

He was probably thinking the same thing she was. Jeb would have immediately responded to the call about a woman being at the end of his road. So why hadn't the kidnapper called Jeb sooner if he'd already released her?

Maybe the person who'd taken Melanie wanted to be certain that he'd have time to get away. After all, Jeb was a former lawman, and it was possible Melanie's abductor hadn't wanted to take a risk that Jeb would spot him. The abductor also wouldn't have wanted anyone else noticing him near where he'd left Melanie. That made sense, but it still left her with two big questions.

Who'd taken Melanie and why?

Yes, taking her had tormented Delaney, but the torment would have been much greater if Melanie had been held captive longer. Each minute would have been agony for both women, and the agony would have been intensified if the kidnapper had taunted Delaney with calls or photos so that she'd know the pain and terror Melanie was going through. That would have been much greater punishment than leaving her assistant on the side of the road.

Of course, the ultimate punishment would have been for the kidnapper to kill Melanie. Delaney was beyond thankful that hadn't happened, but she had to wonder why Webb wouldn't have taken that final step and ended Melanie's life.

"Any idea why this man would have left you near my father's ranch?" Cash asked.

Melanie shook her head again. "Like I said, he didn't talk, and I don't know your father." She paused. "You think he did?" She shifted her gaze to Delaney. "Does Webb know Cash's father?"

"I doubt it. Jeb never visited me when Cash and I were together." Now it was Delaney who paused. "But Jeb was the sheriff of Dark River for a long time. Decades. So it's possible that Webb or Ramone had some kind of run-in with him."

"I'll ask Jeb about that," Cash assured them.

"There's something else," Melanie said, getting Delaney's attention. "I don't know if it's important…"

"Anything you remember could be important," Cash told Melanie when she stopped.

Melanie's bruised forehead bunched up. "I remember his smell," she said. "Strong aftershave. I mean, really strong." She stopped again, probably noticing that both Cash and Delaney had re-acted to that.

"Byers," Cash and Delaney said in unison.

Cash pulled out his phone. "I'll get him in for questioning now."

Chapter Nine

Cash cursed under his breath when he saw the latest text from Jesse. A text to let Cash know that no one had been able to get in touch yet with Byers.

The PI hadn't been in his office and wasn't answering his phone. In fact, no one had seen him since he left Cash's ranch the day before. Cash seriously doubted Byers was the victim of foul play, but it was possible he was avoiding being brought in for questioning.

That was why Cash had issued a BOLO, for everyone to be on the lookout. Cops all over would be keeping an eye out for Byers. If Cash got lucky and the PI was found, he could haul his butt in for an interview as a person of interest in Melanie's abduction. Maybe even for attempted murder in the bombing at Delaney's house.

Cash sipped his third cup of coffee and considered that for a moment. A strong aftershave wasn't exactly compelling evidence, but paired with the fact that Byers had purportedly had an affair with

Webb's lover, it was enough for the BOLO and an official interview.

Not enough for an arrest, though.

Not nearly enough.

Then again, maybe Byers hadn't done anything to warrant an arrest. Maybe this all came back to Ramone or Webb, and perhaps one of them had doused himself with aftershave to make sure Melanie didn't pick up on any other scents that might be linked back to them.

Like the smell of a ranch, for example.

A ranch had some pretty distinct odors, and it was possible Webb had driven Melanie to his brother's ranch, beat her to torment Delaney and then taken her to Jeb's place. But Cash had trouble with that theory. Because there was a piece that just didn't fit.

Why had the kidnapper left Melanie at Jeb's?

That was the question that had gone around in Cash's mind all night, and it had cost him some sleep. Of course, the biggest reason he hadn't slept had been Delaney. She'd stayed in his guest room, and his body hadn't wanted to let him forget that she was just across the hall. But he'd ignored the ache he had for her, because she hadn't needed sex. She'd needed rest, and he was hoping she had gotten more than he had. However, one look at her when she stepped in the kitchen, and he knew that she hadn't.

Wearing loaner jeans and a pale blue shirt that

Cash had gotten from his sister, Delaney went straight to the coffeepot, poured a cup and cooled it down with some tap water so she could chug it like medicine.

"Melanie and I have been emailing this morning," she said, staring down into her cup. "It's early, but she's awake."

It was indeed early, only half past six, and the sun wasn't even up yet. But Cash suspected Melanie hadn't had a peaceful night's sleep, either.

"How's she doing?" Cash asked.

Delaney sighed. "About as well as can be expected, I suppose. She's been sending an email to me about every ten minutes since midnight."

Cash wasn't surprised about the emails. He'd loaned Delaney a laptop and made sure that Melanie had one as well so they could do just that. He figured they needed to have those email chats and that it would help soothe them both. Well, as much as they could be soothed, considering there was a snake who wanted to do Delaney even more harm.

"I've arranged for the safe house for Melanie," Cash told Delaney. "She'll be moved there once doctors release her."

Hopefully, a release that wouldn't happen until Melanie had agreed to speak to a counselor. The kind of trauma she'd gone through could eat away at her if she didn't get help.

It was the same for Delaney.

Cash was still deciding the best way to convince

her to speak to a professional. She'd probably fight it after the experience she'd had with the reaction to the meds, but she needed it to get past what had happened. What she needed more, however, was safety, and that was at the top of Cash's to-do list.

"I thought you might come to my room last night," she said, finally lifting her gaze from her coffee to meet his.

"Trust me, I considered it. *Strongly considered it*," he emphasized. "But I thought you needed rest more than you needed me."

Delaney didn't jump to agree with him about that, and it gave his body a very bad message. A message that Delaney might need him to the point where he could haul her off to bed.

With both hands still wrapped around her mug, she went to him. Her eyes never left his when she leaned down and kissed him. Even though he'd seen it coming, the jolt of it still hit him damn hard.

A punch of pure lust.

It was something he often felt for Delaney, but it had a dangerous edge to it now. They were also revved from the danger and looking for an outlet to deal with the fact they'd nearly been killed in the bombing. But Cash didn't want to be an outlet. Not when it could cost them focus.

And more.

There was that whole issue with Delaney's father. Cash could dive into the kiss headfirst. Could probably do that hauling her off to bed as well. But doing those things would come with a huge price tag, and he wasn't sure he should just offer up his heart for another stomping. Still, he didn't pull back, *couldn't* pull back, when Delaney deepened the kiss.

That tore down any shred of resistance, and Cash put aside his coffee cup so he could hook an arm around her and draw her even closer to him. Mouth to mouth and breath to breath. She didn't make any attempt to move away from him. Just the opposite. She practically dropped her cup on the table next to his, slid her hands around his neck and kept on kissing him.

Cash forgot all about high price tags, stomped-on hearts and clouded judgment. Hell, he wasn't sure he could even think straight, but he knew something for certain. He wanted Delaney, and he was willing to pay whatever price there was to have her.

Obviously, Delaney was dealing with her own needs for him, because she moved right onto his lap when Cash guided her there. Now they were kissing and touching. A lethal combination for foreplay, but this felt a whole lot more than just foreplay.

She tasted hot. Like things forbidden. Things he should resist. But wouldn't. Couldn't. And she felt as good as she tasted. Her body trembled beneath his touch, and her breath hitched when he slid his hand down the front of her shirt to cup her breasts.

Cash had been out of it when they'd done all the touching and kissing two nights ago after she'd shown up at his house. But he wasn't out of it now.

He was feeling and taking everything in. Her silky skin. Her scent. The little sounds of need that were coming from her throat.

He got more of those sounds when he flicked his thumb over her nipple, and she pressed her forehead to his. "I know this is a bad idea."

So did he. Cash wasn't disputing that, but he could justify that a round of good, sweaty sex would clear the air between them. It would burn off some of this aching need they had for each other.

Or not.

It was just as possible that sex would only cause the need to soar, but Cash didn't see he had much of a choice in this. He wanted Delaney, and he wanted her now.

He lowered his arm from her waist to her butt, pushing her center right against his erection. It was a fit that nearly took off the top of his head, and it would have almost certainly led to more kissing and more touching if he hadn't heard the sound over the throbbing in his ears. Not one of Delaney's silky moans of need. No. It was his phone ringing.

Cash cursed the interruption. He wanted to ignore the call and finish things with Delaney. But he couldn't do that. Not with an active investigation where her life was at risk.

"We'll pick this up later," he grumbled. "Promise."

He eased Delaney back, breaking the intimate contact between them. Ignoring the protests of his body and the groan of complaint that Delaney made, he took his phone from his pocket. One look at the screen, and he knew it was a call he'd have to take.

"It's Byers," Cash relayed to Delaney.

She groaned again but moved off his lap as Cash answered the call. He also put it on speaker.

"You put out a BOLO on me?" Byers snarled the moment he was on the line.

"I did." Cash also snarled, and he knew his tone was a heck of a lot meaner. "You're a person of interest in Melanie Adams's kidnapping, and I need to interview you."

That must've stunned Byers into silence, because he didn't make a quick comeback. "What are you talking about?"

"Melanie Adams," Cash repeated, speaking slowly. "She's Delaney's assistant, and you're a person of interest in her abduction and assault."

"You've lost your mind." Byers was back to snarling. "I didn't kidnap her. I don't even know her."

"Well, she knows you." And Cash decided to try to press some of the PI's buttons. "Or rather she got a whiff of you. That aftershave you wear is distinct. You probably should have showered before you kidnapped anyone."

"I didn't kidnap her," Byers practically yelled. "I don't have any reason to do that."

"Oh, yes, you do," Cash argued. "You want to

**Claim up to FOUR NEW BOOKS & TWO MYSTERY GIFTS –
absolutely FREE!**

Dear Reader,

We both know life can be difficult at times. That's why it's important to treat yourself so you can relax and recharge once in a while.

And I'd like to help you do this by sending you this amazing offer of up to FOUR brand new full length FREE BOOKS that WE pay for.

This is everything I have ready to send to you right now:

Try **Harlequin® Romantic Suspense** books featuring heart-racing page-turners with unexpected plot twists and irresistible chemistry that will keep you guessing to the very end.

Try **Harlequin Intrigue® Larger-Print** books featuring action-packed stories that will keep you on the edge of your seat. Solve the crime and deliver justice at all costs.

Or **TRY BOTH!**

All we ask in return is that you answer 4 simple questions on the attached Treat Yourself survey. You'll get **Two Free Books** and **Two Mystery Gifts** from each series you try, *altogether worth over $20!* Who could pass up a deal like that?

Sincerely,

Pam Powers

Harlequin Reader Service

Treat Yourself to Free Books and Free Gifts.

Answer 4 fun questions and get rewarded.

▶ DETACH AND MAIL CARD TODAY! ▶

	YES	NO
1. I LOVE reading a good book.		
2. I indulge and "treat" myself often.		
3. I love getting FREE things.		
4. Reading is one of my favorite activities.		

TREAT YOURSELF • Pick your 2 Free Books...

Yes! Please send me my Free Books from each series I select and Free Mystery Gifts. I understand that I am under no obligation to buy anything, as explained on the back of this card.

Which do you prefer?

❏ **Harlequin® Romantic Suspense** 240/340 HDL GRCZ
❏ **Harlequin Intrigue® Larger-Print** 199/399 HDL GRCZ
❏ **Try Both** 240/340 & 199/399 HDL GRDD

FIRST NAME   LAST NAME

ADDRESS

APT.#   CITY

STATE/PROV.   ZIP/POSTAL CODE

EMAIL ❏ Please check this box if you would like to receive newsletters and promotional emails from Harlequin Enterprises ULC and its affiliates. You can unsubscribe anytime.

© 2022 HARLEQUIN ENTERPRISES ULC
™ and ® are trademarks owned by Harlequin Enterprises ULC. Printed in the U.S.A.

HI/HRS-520-TY22

If offer card is missing write to: Harlequin Reader Service, P.O. Box 1341, Buffalo, NY 14240-8531 or visit www.ReaderService.com

BUSINESS REPLY MAIL
FIRST-CLASS MAIL PERMIT NO. 717 BUFFALO, NY

POSTAGE WILL BE PAID BY ADDRESSEE

HARLEQUIN READER SERVICE
PO BOX 1341
BUFFALO NY 14240-8571

NO POSTAGE
NECESSARY
IF MAILED
IN THE
UNITED STATES

get back at Delaney. But I can't figure out if that's because she fired you or because you despise her."

"That's nonsense—"

"Beatrice Stockwell," Cash interrupted, stopping what would have no doubt been a tirade. And, yeah, it stopped Byers, all right.

"What about her?" Byers asked. The snarl was gone, and in its place was a quiet kind of concern.

Cash had no intention of ratting out Beatrice's friend Sasha. He couldn't be certain that Byers wouldn't fly off the handle and go after the woman. So he kept things simple.

"You had an affair with Beatrice." Cash stated it as fact. "An affair that was going on while she was still living with Webb. Don't bother to lie and deny it because I have proof. That's why there's a BOLO out on you. That's why you'll be coming in for questioning. First, by me, but I'm betting the FBI will want in on this."

There was a long silence, and Cash would have loved to see Byers's expression. Part of him wished he'd waited to drop this at the interview, but Cash hadn't been sure that Byers would actually show up in Clay Ridge. Byers might just go on the run. If he did, at least Cash would have had this chance to confront him. To let Byers know that he was sussing out the reason the PI was so adamant about Delaney being guilty of sending that threatening letter.

"Yes, I had a relationship with Beatrice," Byers

finally said. "But that has nothing to do with Delaney or her assistant."

"You're sure about that?" Cash taunted. "Because I have a theory that you're riled about Delaney not getting Webb acquitted of the murder charges. And I think you're riled because in your guilty little mind, you know Webb is innocent. You know that because you're the one who murdered Beatrice."

"I did not," Byers shouted, and he spewed out a string of profanities. Cash just let the man wind himself down. "I didn't kill anyone. Webb murdered Beatrice, and I wanted justice for her. Justice that didn't happen because that SOB Ramone is a free man."

Bingo. There it was. The little nugget that Cash had been waiting to hear. Obviously, Delaney had, too, because she was staring at the phone. She released a long, hard breath.

"That sounds like motive for the attacks and threats against Delaney," Cash told Byers. "Ramone is free, and you want revenge. You've decided that Delaney is the target of your revenge."

Again, there was a long silence. "Are you going to arrest me?" Byers came out and asked.

"That depends on what you say during your interview. I want you at the Clay Ridge PD at one o'clock this afternoon. If you're not there, I'll get a warrant for your apprehension and arrest."

"I'll be there," Byers snapped. "With my lawyers. You're not getting away with this, *Sheriff.* I won't be your scapegoat."

Byers ended the call abruptly. No surprise there. Cash hadn't expected the PI to stay on the line as long as he had. A smart man would have ended the call the moment he realized he was in legal hot water.

"You really believe Byers could have been the one who killed Beatrice?" Delaney asked.

Cash heard the slight tremble in her voice. Saw the worry in her eyes. Not worry for Byers. But worry because Webb might have been innocent after all. And she would blame herself for an innocent man being sent to prison.

He stood, went to her and pulled her into his arms. This wasn't the hot and fast embrace when she'd been on his lap. He hoped his arms would give her some comfort. What he had to say possibly could, too.

"There was enough evidence to convict Webb," he reminded her. "You didn't send him to jail. A jury did."

She nodded, sighed. "As his lawyer, I really did do everything I could to make sure he wasn't convicted."

"I know you did."

And because she needed it, he kissed her again. Yes, this was for comfort, but still he deepened it. It didn't send them into the rush to haul each other off to bed, but when he eased back, Cash was pleased that she was a little breathless.

"Better?" he asked.

"Your kisses don't make things better," she muttered.

"Ouch," Cash joked. Well, partially joked. It did sting.

"I mean they don't make this better." She motioned toward his phone. "Your kisses make me wish all was well, that Melanie hadn't been hurt and that we could be cocooned in our own bed."

That took away some of the sting, and he smiled. Kissed her again. Too bad they couldn't do the cocoon thing because his body was still aching for her. He probably would have tried to soothe that ache with another kiss, but his blasted phone rang again. Some of his annoyance vanished, though, when he saw Jesse's name on the screen. His deputy could be calling because of trouble.

"Is everything okay?" Cash asked the moment he answered.

"I just got a call from Lubbock PD," Jesse explained. "They canvassed Delaney's neighbors after the bombing, and they all claim they didn't see anything suspicious. But one of her neighbors pulled a double shift at work, and didn't hear about the bombing until he got home. He called the cops a little while ago to tell them he had seen someone go into Delaney's house."

Cash latched on to the hope that this could be

the break they needed to ID Webb. "Please tell me the neighbor got a good look at the guy."

"Oh, he did," Jesse verified. "He said he thought the guy could be there for repairs or such, but that he got a bad feeling about it. That's why he took out his phone and snapped a picture."

"A picture," Delaney repeated in a whisper, and there was plenty of hope in her voice, too.

"I'm sending you the image now," Jesse explained.

A moment later, Cash's phone dinged, and the photo loaded. He enlarged it, zooming right in on the man who was at Delaney's front door. The guy's head was turned, as if he was looking around for someone who might spot him, and the angle gave them a good view of the man's face.

Hell.

Chapter Ten

Delaney could have sworn her heart stopped. It just stopped. And the breath rushed from her body.

Because it was a picture of her father.

"When was the photo taken?" Cash asked Jesse.

"About two hours before the bomb went off," his deputy promptly answered, which told Delaney it was a question he'd already asked Lubbock PD.

She frantically picked through the memory of the conversation Cash and she had had with her father, and recalled that Gil hadn't said anything about going to her house during that time.

Nothing.

Gil had told them he'd come to her house to leave a note, because he was worried about her, but he hadn't said anything about going there two hours earlier. But maybe he had done just that and then had forgotten to mention it.

"Does the neighbor know if Gil actually went into the house?" Cash pressed.

"He said he did. The neighbor considered calling

the cops then and there, but he said the guy had a key, so he figured it was okay."

Cash looked at her, and she understood what he wanted to know. Did her father have a key? "Yes, he had a spare key," Delaney answered.

"The neighbor isn't sure how long Delaney's father stayed in the house," Jesse went on, "but he was still inside when the neighbor left for work. The neighbor estimates that was at least ten minutes, because he was watching out the window while he was having his coffee."

Cash muttered something that she didn't catch and scrubbed his hand over his face. His expression was a mix of dread and frustration. And she knew why. Even if her father had done nothing wrong, Cash was still going to have to talk to him. That wouldn't be pleasant for any of them.

"See if Lubbock PD will give you the neighbor's name so Delaney and I can talk to him," Cash told his deputy. "I'll get it touch with Gil now and see what he has to say about all of this."

Cash ended the call with Jesse and handed her his phone. "Go ahead and press in your dad's number. If he hears my voice first, he might just hang up."

She couldn't argue with that. He probably wouldn't take a call from Cash. But there was the possibility Gil would do the same to her. Their conversation at her house hadn't ended all that well. Still, that wasn't going to stand in the way of getting the answers they needed. She had to know why her father had gone into her house and if he'd seen that threat that'd been painted on her wall.

Or if he'd been the one to leave the threat.

Delaney pushed that disturbing possibility aside and pressed in Gil's number. She held her breath, waited, but he didn't answer. Not on the first ring, the second or even the third. Finally, he picked up. Except it wasn't her father.

"Trevor Salvetti," the PI greeted.

Since Delaney hadn't expected him to answer, it took her a couple of seconds to regroup. "This is Delaney. I need to speak to my father."

"Welcome to the club," Salvetti muttered. "I was about to call you to let you know that your father sneaked out during the night."

"Where is he?" Delaney blurted out.

"I have no idea. He left his phone, probably so it couldn't be traced. I don't even know when he left. Around midnight, he said he was headed to bed, and he went to his room. When I didn't hear him stirring this morning, I went to check on him, and he was gone."

Delaney wanted to curse. Or yell. The reason she'd hired a PI was so her father would be safe, and now he wasn't. In fact, it was possible that something horrible had happened to him.

"Could Webb have kidnapped him?" Delaney came out and asked. As much as she hated to hear the answer, she had to know.

"I don't think so. There's no sign of a struggle, and it appears he went out through the window in his bedroom." The PI groaned. "I'm so sorry about this. Gil didn't show any signs of running, or I would have kept a closer watch on him."

Her father had no doubt purposely made sure not to telegraph any moves to make the PI suspicious. But why had he run?

And better yet, where the heck was he?

"Did Gil take his truck?" Cash asked, and then he identified himself so that the PI would know he was talking to a cop.

"No. It's still here. Unless he had another vehicle stashed somewhere nearby, he left on foot."

That only caused Delaney's fears to skyrocket. Her father lived over two miles outside of town, and if he'd walked, Webb could have spotted him and taken him. Of course, there was no proof that Webb was actually after Gil, and Delaney had to hang on to that. If she didn't, the panic was going to eat away at her until she couldn't think straight.

"Did your father ever mention that he's had blackouts?" Salvetti asked.

"No," she answered without hesitating. If he had, she would have remembered. "I know he still drinks, and sometimes he passes out from it."

"It's more than that," Salvetti said. "We were talking last night before he went to bed, and he told me he'd had a couple of blackouts, times when he'd woken up and didn't know how he'd gotten there."

Sweet heaven. That terrified her even more. "Could that have happened last night? Could he have had so much to drink that he left the house without realizing what he was doing?"

"I doubt it. I couldn't find any bottles of booze in his room. Plus, if he'd been drunk, I doubt he would have made such a clean getaway. He probably would have stumbled or even fallen when he crawled out the window."

That was true. Her father wouldn't have gotten drunk and then cleaned up the liquor bottles. Still, that didn't rule out foul play. After all, Webb had managed to break in through her office to get to Melanie. Webb could have done the same at her father's house, especially since Gil didn't even have a security system.

"I'm taking his phone and heading out to look for him now," the PI explained. "If I spot him, I'll call you. It would help if you could text me the names of any friends he might have gone to."

"He doesn't have any friends," Delaney said on a sigh. It sounded pitiful, but it was the truth. "I can give you the contact info for his boss."

"I've got that, and I'll drive over to the ranch and ask if anyone's seen him." The PI paused. "If Gil's actually on the run, though, he probably wouldn't go where he knows we'd look."

True. And that meant he could be anywhere. Midnight was hours ago, so he could have already had at least a six-hour head start. He could have gotten into Lubbock, and from there, ended up heaven knew where.

"Any idea how much money Gil would have had on hand?" Salvetti asked.

"Probably not much," Delaney admitted. "I think he lives pretty much paycheck to paycheck." Still, he could have squirreled away enough for a hotel or a bus ticket. But that brought her back around full circle.

Why would he have done that?

Why would he have run from the PI she'd hired to protect him? Or maybe her father was actually running from her.

"Call me if you hear from him or find out where he is," Delaney emphasized, and she ended the call so she could hand Cash back his phone.

Cash sat there, the muscles tight on his face and with a hitch in his breathing. Like her, he was obviously trying to work out Gil's motive for running, and judging from the profanity he muttered, he wasn't having any better luck with that than she had. Or maybe Cash had come up with a reason he knew she wasn't going to like.

"I need to get someone over to your father's house," Cash finally said. "A cop, maybe a CSI."

Her chest suddenly got very tight. "You think Webb kidnapped him?"

Cash looked her straight in the eyes. "It's possible that Webb lured him out…"

"But?" she prompted when he stopped and muttered another curse.

He took a deep breath before he continued. "I also need to know if there are any signs that Gil built a bomb in his house."

Delaney had no choice. She dropped down into the chair. Because if she hadn't, she would have fallen flat on her face.

"I'm not saying for sure that Gil blew up your house," Cash continued. "But it's something that needs to be ruled out."

She managed a headshake. "Why would you even consider he's done this?"

Cash slid his hand over hers. "Because of the timing of that text I got. *If you want to find me, go to Delaney's house*," he recited. *"I left something that oughta give her a nightmare or two."*

Delaney felt another wave of fear slide over her. "Webb sent that text," she murmured.

"Maybe. Probably," Cash amended. "But I have to rule out that your father sent it to lure me to your house so I'd be there when the bomb went off. I need to question him, Delaney," he quickly added. "I need to bring him in for an official interview."

"Like Byers," she said. Mercy, it felt as if her throat had clamped shut, making it hard for her to breathe. "They're both suspects."

"They're both persons of interest who I need to rule out," he corrected.

But there was a flip side to that, and Delaney

knew it. If he couldn't rule them out, then they were indeed suspects.

"Even if you find my father, he won't want you to interview him," she reminded Cash.

Cash nodded. "I'll have Jesse or one of the other deputies do it. But first, we have to find him." He texted Jesse, and Delaney saw that Cash was requesting a BOLO on her father.

"You really believe there's a possibility that my father could have wanted to kill you?" she asked. Delaney tried to tamp down the tremble in her voice. And she tried to blink back the tears that were threatening to spill.

"You tell me," he said. Not as a challenge. His voice was gentle. His words, a plea for her to go back through that conversation they'd had outside her house.

She got up, went to the window and stared out while she considered everything she'd just learned. Her father's blackouts. Him leaving his phone behind. The anger that had been in his voice and on his face when he'd confronted them at her house. And there was no doubt about it—that had been a confrontation. Then, there were his own words.

I can't go through this again.

I can't watch this happen.

Had her father's hatred for Cash and the possibility of them getting back together sent Gil over the edge? As much as it twisted away at her, there was only one answer. An answer she had to give Cash.

"Yes, it's possible," she admitted.

She stood there, watching the beautiful sunrise come up over the pastures. A beauty that didn't ease the ache inside her one bit. Because, yes, it was possible.

And more.

Much more.

Had her father also left that horrible message for her on the foyer wall? She didn't want to believe it was possible, but Delaney couldn't put blinders on and hope that he was innocent. That way of thinking could get Cash killed. Because if her father had truly lost it, then she wouldn't be his first target.

Cash would.

She was trying so hard to fight back those blasted tears that she didn't hear Cash walk up behind her. However, she felt his arms when they went around her. This embrace didn't have the heat, but it was very much needed. Cash had always been a rock for her, and right now, she needed someone to lean on so she could get through this. She'd need him even more if it turned out that her father had intended to kill.

"I swear, I won't read anything into what you're doing right now," she said, pressing the back of her head to the crook of his neck.

She felt him go a little stiff. "What do you mean?"

"This." She ran her hand over his arm. The arm that was giving her so much comfort. "I know you're caught up in the emotion of us nearly being killed, but it doesn't erase what I did to you."

He didn't ask her to clarify what she was referring to. No need. She'd crushed Cash when she'd ended their engagement, and she hadn't told him the truth of why she'd done it, because she hadn't wanted him to confront her father. It was only going to make this situation more bitter if it turned out that Gil was the one behind the attacks.

"You still have feelings for me," he threw out there.

She did. No doubts about that. But it was more than feelings. Delaney was still in love with him, but now wasn't the time to drop that bombshell on him. Especially since it could mess things up even more than they already were.

Cash's phone rang again, the sound slicing through the silence. And the moment. Cash eased back and frowned when he saw the screen.

"It's from Dark River PD," he muttered.

Delaney whirled around, her attention going straight to his phone because this could be about Melanie. Thankfully, Cash put the call on speaker.

"Sheriff Mercer," the woman said when Cash answered. "I'm Deputy Dawn Farley. I work for your sister, and I'm on guard duty at the hospital. We've had an, uh, incident."

"Is Melanie all right?" Delaney blurted out.

"I'm guessing you're Melanie's boss?" the deputy asked.

"Yes, I'm Delaney Archer," she snapped, annoyed that she had to wait even a second for what could be critical info. "Is Melanie all right?" Delaney repeated.

"She's safe," Deputy Farley assured her.

That should have at least helped Delaney tamp down the surge of adrenaline, but it didn't. "What kind of incident?"

"Someone sent her flowers," the deputy answered after a heavy sigh, "and the card said—and I'm quoting—*I'm not finished with you. Let's play again real soon.*"

Oh, mercy. Delaney's legs went weak again, and she steadied herself by leaning against the kitchen counter. But she also felt something more than the wobbliness and the fresh adrenaline. There was anger. Hot and raw. Because Melanie didn't deserve to be put through this.

"Who delivered the flowers?" Cash asked.

"A man named Noah Carson. He's not much more than a kid, Sheriff. And he's not behind the threat. He's just the person who makes deliveries. But get this, the person who ordered the flowers didn't do it over the phone. It was a man, and he did it in person at a Lubbock florist. He came in last night right before the shop was due to close, and he asked that the flowers be delivered first thing this morning."

Everything inside Delaney tightened. Because she was afraid the deputy was about to say her father had placed the order. But Delaney just couldn't see him making that kind of threat. If Gil was behind the attacks, then he'd have no reason to taunt her with Melanie.

"Please tell me you've got a good description of the man," Cash said.

"I've got a good description," Deputy Farley verified. "Your sister had a couple of Lubbock uniforms go to the florist, and after hearing the clerk describe the guy, they showed her Webb's picture. The clerk says she's about ninety percent sure that Webb was the one who bought the flowers."

Delaney got a quick hit of relief that it hadn't been her father, but the relief vanished as fast as it had come. Because this was proof that Webb was alive. Alive and trying to make her life a living hell by using someone like Melanie.

"Are there security cameras in the flower shop?" Cash asked.

"No. But Lubbock PD is checking to see if Webb appeared on any of the cameras from nearby shops. He paid cash," the deputy continued, "so he didn't leave a paper trail, but the clerk said when he left he got into a black truck that he'd parked right out front. Sorry, he didn't get a look at the plates, but he noticed a big crack across the front of the windshield."

That wasn't the best of descriptions when trying to track down a killer, but maybe it'd be enough for someone at Lubbock PD to spot the truck. And Webb.

"Which direction was Webb heading when he left?" Cash pressed.

"East," the deputy readily provided. "But there's a big intersection less than a half mile from the florist. Lubbock PD will have a look at traffic cams. We might get lucky."

Yes, and they desperately needed some luck. "Please don't let Webb get to Melanie again," Delaney said.

"I won't. But this will probably speed up her going to the safe house. She's just too spooked to stay here, and I don't blame her. It'll be a lot easier to keep Webb away if we're not in a hospital where there are plenty of strangers coming and going."

Delaney agreed. She just hoped that Melanie was well enough to make the trip.

"Keep me posted about anything Lubbock PD finds on those cams," Cash added to the deputy before he ended the call.

"I won't be able to see Melanie once she's at the safe house, will I?" Delaney asked him.

Cash shook his head. "It'd be too dangerous. If Webb managed to follow us there, it could put both you and Melanie in danger."

She'd known that was what he would say, but it still gnawed away at her. Melanie had gotten hurt because of her, and Delaney wouldn't even be able to comfort her. Then again, maybe that was for the best. She wasn't sure how much comfort she could give when every nerve in her body was firing on all cylinders.

Delaney tried to calm those nerves so she could process all the info spinning in her head. Webb's sighting meant he was definitely involved in Melanie's kidnapping. More involved in everything that had happened. If she went with that theory, then Webb had been the one who'd left that message for her in the foyer. So maybe her father's visit meant nothing.

Except that he hadn't said anything about it.

Maybe his visit had been part of one of his blackouts? She prayed that was it. Because a blackout was far better than the alternative, that her father had plotted to murder Cash and had nearly gotten them both killed in the process.

"I want to go ahead and update Curley about this," Cash said, drawing her attention back to him. He went through his dispatcher to get the agent's number and made the call.

Curley answered right away, and Cash filled him in on the flowers. And then told him about her father's disappearance.

"I can help," Curley volunteered. "Let me see if I can speed up the process of getting that traffic cam feed. I can also nudge a few contacts to try to get someone out looking for Gil." He paused. "You think he left because he's guilty of something?"

That was the million-dollar question. Too bad Delaney didn't know the answer.

"I need to rule him out," Cash said. "Ditto for Byers. I need to make sure they didn't have a part in this."

"Can't say about Delaney's father," Curley answered, "but something popped on Byers."

"What?" Cash and she asked in unison.

"I got access to Delaney's medical report on her allergic reaction to the medication."

Of all the things Delaney had thought the agent might say, that wasn't one of them. "Why?"

"Because I didn't like the timing," Curley readily admitted. "I just thought it was too pat that you'd have that reaction right about the time Webb was taunting you with those threats."

"I agree," Cash said. "What'd you find out, and how does this connect to Byers?"

"According to the doctor who treated Delaney after she collapsed, he thought she'd taken some kind of drug that caused disorientation and maybe hallucinations. The lab results that just came back confirmed it. It was a strong anti-seizure medication."

Delaney frantically shook her head. "I don't have seizures, and I didn't take anything like that."

"Not knowingly," Curley agreed. "But I believe someone switched your meds. You had the bottle in your office, right?"

"That's right. I keep it in my center desk drawer, and I have another bottle at home." And she stopped. Because Melanie's kidnapper had broken in through her office. Webb or someone else had also gotten into Delaney's home to leave that message in the foyer. If he'd done that once, he could have done it to replace the meds.

Her stomach was twisting and knotting again, too, and it sickened her to think that someone had not only broken in but had tampered with her meds. The person who'd done that could have killed her.

So why hadn't he?

Because this was yet more taunting? In this case, it had gone well beyond that because she'd ended up in the hospital.

"So why do you think Byers is connected?" Delaney asked the agent.

"Because he does have seizures," Curley explained. "And the specific medication that was in your system is the one he's been prescribed."

Chapter Eleven

Cash ended the call with Agent Curley, and he did the only thing he could do. He pulled Delaney into his arms and tried to give her what comfort he could. Which probably wasn't much.

Every detail they learned had to feel like another blow to her. Webb, Byers or whoever the hell was doing this was nipping away at her. Bite after greedy bite. Cash wanted to promise her that he'd end these taunts. The threat. But first he had to learn who was responsible.

"Byers," Delaney said with her head on his shoulder.

Yes, Byers was definitely high on the suspect list, but Cash didn't want to zoom in only on the PI. Shifting the investigation solely to Byers could turn out to be a big mistake along with letting a killer get a chance at, well, killing.

"Webb could have stolen Byers's meds and put them in your pill bottle," Cash pointed out.

Her father could have done that as well, but Cash

couldn't see Gil going in that direction. If Gil was the culprit, then Delaney wasn't the target. Cash was. But that didn't mean it wasn't her father who set the explosive. Webb could be the one responsible for everything else.

"It's possible that Webb even knew about Byers's seizures," Cash went on. "We don't know if Beatrice told Webb anything about her side lover."

Delaney eased back, her eyes meeting his, and she nodded. "If Webb found out about the affair, he could have beaten or threatened her until she gave him info about Byers. Once Webb had a name, he'd be able to do some research." But she stopped and shook her head. "It's not easy to hack into medical records."

"He wouldn't have had to hack. It was several days before Webb was arrested for Beatrice's murder, and Webb could have used that time to stalk Byers. He maybe even broken into Byers's office or home. He could have broken in again after he escaped jail and stolen some of the meds then. Byers might not have even noticed."

Delaney stayed quiet a moment, obviously trying to work that through, and she finally nodded. Then she sighed. It wasn't a weak sound, though. It had some anger in it.

"Webb is playing a very sick game," she said. Her voice was no longer shaky. "And I want him to pay for everything he's done."

Cash couldn't agree more. He just hoped he

could find Webb before the man could do any more damage. Ditto for finding her father. For starters, though, maybe he could get some answers from Byers when he interviewed him at one.

And that brought Cash to another concern.

"I can get one of my deputies to interview Byers," he said. "But I'd prefer to do it myself."

"Of course," she readily agreed. "I want to be there. I want to hear what he has to say, especially when you ask him about the meds."

Cash wasn't surprised that she'd want to be in on that. After all, those meds had caused her all kinds of trouble. But being at the interview could be trouble, too.

"We could be attacked on the road," he pointed out. "In fact, Webb might be waiting for us to drive to the station."

Delaney paused only a heartbeat. "I still want to be there."

Cash wasn't surprised by that, either. There was plenty enough fight in Delaney for her to want to see this through to the end. But he was going to have to take some serious precautions, and that started with a call to Jesse so Cash could get backup for the drive. However, before he could contact his deputy, his phone rang, and this time the name and number on the screen were familiar.

"It's Leigh," he relayed to Delaney. "Please tell me you have good news," Cash added to his sister once he'd answered the call.

"Well, it's news. Not sure you'll think it's good, though."

That caused Cash to groan. "What is it?"

"Lubbock PD got a fast hit from the traffic cams on that black truck with the cracked windshield. The one Webb got in outside the florist," she added. "The cams picked it up a couple of times, and they got a good enough image to confirm that it was Webb behind the wheel."

Even though Cash had expected the news, it still packed a wallop. And it confirmed that Webb had a part in at least the threats and the taunts.

"The plates are bogus," Leigh went on. "No surprise there. I suspect it's also stolen and that Webb will be ditching it soon."

Cash figured the same thing. Webb had to have known there was the possibility that he'd be spotted on camera. Heck, he probably wanted that since it played into the fear he was trying to build for Delaney. But now that he'd been spotted, Webb couldn't risk the cops noticing those bogus tags and pulling him over.

"There's more," Leigh continued a moment later. "The last of the traffic cams show that Webb took the exit that could lead to Clay Ridge. *Could,*" she emphasized. "He could have gone up a mile or two and circled back. He might not be anywhere near Clay Ridge right now."

No, but Cash had the sickening feeling that Webb would eventually end up here. After all, Webb meant to come after her. If he didn't have confirmation that Delaney was indeed in Clay Ridge, then he could easily find out.

"Uh, one more thing," Leigh said a moment later. "You'll hear it sooner or later, so I wanted you to hear it from me. I'm engaged to Cullen Brodie."

Cash didn't laugh. Or groan. But a couple of months ago, that was exactly what he would have done. There was a long-standing feud between the Brodies and the Mercers. It was a Texas version of the Hatfields and McCoys. There was no way in hell that Jeb or Cullen's father, Bowen, would approve of such an engagement, but Leigh and Cullen had obviously managed to put that aside.

Something that Cash wished Delaney could do.

Her father's bad blood was with Jeb, but Cash doubted Bowen would be thinking suicide over his son's engagement to Jeb's daughter. Nope. Bowen would just be pissed off, maybe even disown Cullen, but obviously Leigh and Cullen hadn't allowed that possibility to get in the way of Cullen popping the question and Leigh accepting.

"Congrats," Cash told his sister. "You're happy?"

"Yes," Leigh said so fast that it caused Cash to smile. His sister wasn't known for her big displays of affection. Probably because she'd learned to hide her feelings from all the hurt Jeb had caused. "I love Cullen," she added, sounding very much like an over-the-moon bride-to-be.

"I'm happy for you," Delaney muttered, drawing Cash's attention back to her.

Oh, man. There was hurt in her eyes, and he knew it went back to their own engagement. The one she'd broken to save her father. Delaney was probably indeed happy for his sister, but this brought back the old painful memories. Not just for Delaney but for him, too.

"Thanks," Leigh answered. "For about two seconds, I considered not accepting Cullen's proposal because I knew the trouble it'd cause for our families. Just for about two seconds." She paused. "But I'm not giving up Cullen over bad feelings that should have been put to rest years ago."

Leigh didn't add that she thought it was something they, too, should consider, but Cash could almost hear the words come out of his sister's mouth. Wise words, indeed. And it almost felt like a personal challenge to Cash, for him to find a way to have Delaney back in his life and not have it ruin her relationship with Gil.

"I'll call you if I get anything else on the traffic cams," Leigh assured Delaney before ending the call.

Cash put his phone away, took a deep breath and looked up at Delaney. She still wasn't rock-solid, but it was probably best if he didn't hug her again right now. The air seemed charged between them. It was practically zinging with emotions, and yes, heat. Best to keep his hands and mouth off her and dive into the work.

"I want to go through all the reports from Lubbock PD," he explained. "I need to find out if their bomb experts have been able to get anything from the explosives that blew up your house."

She nodded. "You mean like a bomber's signature."

That was indeed what he meant. There wouldn't be trace or fibers. Not likely anyway. But bomb makers often had a specific style that could sometimes be used to ID them. It was possible that Webb had made the bomb, but since he didn't have any experience in that area, he could have hired someone. Someone with a signature. If they found the person who'd made the bomb, it could lead them to Webb.

"What can I do to help?" Delaney asked. "Give me something to do," she amended. "I can't just sit around here and do nothing."

He understood that. Cash didn't want too much thinking time for anything other than the investigation. "You can read the reports from your neighbors as to what they saw and didn't see yesterday before that bomb went off. Maybe something one of them said will ring a bell."

It was a long shot, but right now everything they had fell into that particular category.

Cash set up Delaney with a laptop at the kitchen table. However, they'd barely gotten started when his phone rang again. Not Leigh this time but rather Stoney, his ranch hand.

"You got a visitor," Stoney said when Cash answered.

"Not Byers," he grumbled. And if it was the PI, Cash intended to arrest him.

"No. It's your new neighbor." There was plenty of disdain in Stoney's voice. "Ramone Bennison's here."

That sent Cash and Delaney to the living room so they could look out the front window. It was indeed Ramone, and he was sitting in his truck in Cash's driveway. Stoney and his son were there, too, and both were armed with rifles.

"What the heck does he want?" Cash asked.

"He said he needs to talk to you, and that it's real important," Stoney answered. "Ramone said he's got something to tell you about his brother."

DELANEY STARED AT Ramone, who was staring back at them. He didn't have the dogs with him this time, and it appeared he was alone in the truck. Of course, she couldn't help but think that maybe he had hired thugs—or Webb—hiding low on the seat.

But an attack like that would be stupid.

After all, Cash was armed and so were the two ranch hands who were keeping their attention nailed to Ramone. If Ramone was foolish enough to try to fire shots at them, he'd soon be a dead man.

Cash was studying Ramone, too, and he swore

under his breath. "Did he happen to say why he didn't just call me with this *real important* information?" he asked Stoney.

"I asked, and he said this needed to be face-to-face," Stoney answered. "You want me to send him on his way or insist he call you?"

Cash stayed quiet a moment, obviously considering that, and while he was still thinking it over, Ramone stepped out from his truck. He put his hands in the air, maybe to show them he wasn't armed. Or at least he didn't have hold of a weapon, but that didn't mean he wasn't carrying.

"Webb called me," Ramone shouted, looking straight at Cash. "You need to hear what he had to say."

"He's not coming in the house," Cash concluded several long moments later. "And you're not going out there with me."

Delaney caught on to his arm. "But you're going out there?"

"Yeah." Maybe because of the sudden alarm on her face, he brushed a kiss on her mouth and added, "Not in the yard. I'll have Ramone come to the porch."

That would prevent a sniper from getting an easy shot, but there was still the possibility that Cash could be gunned down.

"You can demand that Ramone meet you at your office this afternoon," she suggested. "If he has info about Webb, then it'd be obstruction for him to refuse to tell you."

Cash made a quick sound of agreement. "But I don't want to wait hours to hear what he has to say. He could give me something now that could get Webb back behind bars."

Delaney couldn't dispute that. It was entirely possible that Ramone would indeed want his brother back in jail. But it was also possible that brotherly ties ran deep enough that Ramone would help Webb. Maybe by feeding them false information. Maybe by helping Webb kill Cash by drawing him out into the open.

"I'll be careful, and I won't be long," Cash assured her. He dropped another kiss on her mouth. "Move back from the door." He tipped his head to the kitchen. "Wait in there."

She didn't want to wait or leave him, but it wasn't smart for her to be right in the doorway when Cash opened it. Even if it didn't lead to her getting shot, just her mere presence would be a huge distraction for Cash. Right now, she wanted him focused on Ramone so he could hear whatever the man had to say and then come back inside the house.

"Can you leave your phone with me?" Delaney asked since he was still on the line with Stoney. "That way, if you speak up, I'll be able to hear at least some of the conversation."

Cash nodded. "Did you get that, Stoney?" he asked his ranch hand.

"I got it. I'll try to stay turned toward you and our visitor so that Delaney can hear."

Good. It wouldn't guarantee Cash was safe, but at least she'd know what was happening.

Delaney took Cash's phone, and while watching Cash from over her shoulder, she went to the kitchen. The house had an open floor plan, so she saw him as he disarmed the security system and opened the door. She caught just a glimpse of Ramone walking toward the porch before Cash shut the door behind him.

"This had better be important," Cash immediately warned Ramone.

"It is. Webb called me," she heard Ramone say. "I'll give you the number he used, but he said it wouldn't do any good to try to trace it because he was using a burner."

No surprise there. Webb wouldn't be dumb enough to use a phone that could be traced back to him.

Ramone rattled off the number to Cash, and Delaney hurried to the fridge so she could jot it down on the dry-erase board hanging there.

"Webb asked me to help him," Ramone continued. "He said he needed money and a vehicle. I told him I'd help, but that it'd take me an hour or two to get the cash. He's due to call me back in about thirty minutes."

Delaney felt the quick jolt of hope. She hadn't expected for Cash to get much from Ramone, but this could be the beginning of Webb being apprehended.

"Where are you supposed to meet Webb?" Cash demanded.

"He's coming to my ranch later this morning," Ramone said without hesitation. He muttered something she didn't catch. "Look, he's my brother, but I can't get mixed up in this. If I help him, I could end up in jail, and I've just now started to get my life back together."

"Yeah, you would have ended up in jail," Cash verified. "That's why it was smart of you to come to me."

Delaney agreed with that if Ramone was being on the up-and-up. She wasn't sure he was, and it would be a huge risk for Cash to be sucked into meeting Webb when it could all be a trap. Cash had no doubt already considered that, but she figured it was a risk he'd take.

And that twisted her up again.

Cash would put his life on the line to get Webb, to make sure she was safe. But if something went wrong, and he was hurt—

That thought broke off when she heard a sound behind her. The sound of the back door opening.

Delaney whirled around and came face-to-face with her worst nightmare.

Smiling, Webb barged his way inside and put a gun to her head. "Shh," he said, his hot breath raking against her cheek. "Don't say boo, or you'll get lover boy killed."

Chapter Twelve

Cash studied Ramone's expression and body language. Looking for any signs that the man was lying. If he was, he was darn good at it, because Cash only saw the nerves and the face of a very troubled man.

"Webb's calling you back to confirm you have the money and the vehicle?" Cash asked.

Ramone nodded. "And then his plan is to drive to my place. He said he wants to ditch the truck he has now because the cops know about it."

Yeah, they knew all right, but it still made Cash wonder why Webb had parked and driven the truck so that it could be caught on the security cams. If that had been his plan all along, then why had he waited to call his brother and ask for another vehicle? Why hadn't Webb set that in motion before the florist? Or just skipped a personal appearance at the florist altogether?

Something definitely wasn't right.

"I figured I'd tell Webb that it was okay to come and get the money and a truck," Ramone continued. He kept his gaze pinned to Cash, but Cash did some glancing around, to make sure this wasn't a ploy for Webb to get in position to gun him down. "But maybe you and some of your deputies could be there to take him when he shows up. *Take him alive*," Ramone emphasized. "I don't want to be the reason my brother gets killed."

Cash couldn't give him guarantees about that. Webb would almost certainly be armed, maybe with a gun that he'd gotten from Ramone. Maybe one he'd stolen. Either way, Webb wouldn't just give up in a peaceful surrender.

"Webb knows that Delaney's been staying here," Ramone added. "And no, I didn't tell him. He might have guessed or somebody could have told him."

Any of those were possibilities. Webb might have also had them under surveillance when they were at her house. It wouldn't have been hard to figure out she was staying with him if Webb had seen them together.

"I don't want him going after Delaney." Ramone groaned, shook his head. "I don't want another dead woman on my conscience." He stopped, his eyes widening as if he'd said too much.

Which he had.

Ramone had just come close to confessing that he'd been an accessory to murder. But since he'd already been tried and acquitted for any part in Beatrice's death, double jeopardy applied, and he couldn't be tried for it again.

"Call me once you have everything set up with Webb," Cash instructed. "We'll work out the details as to how to handle this. Tell him not to come through for at least three hours because I need some time to prepare."

That included making sure Delaney was safe, because Cash didn't want this sting operation to be an opportunity for Webb to try to get to her. The moment that thought entered his head, Cash could have sworn someone put ice in his veins.

"Stay here," Cash ordered Ramone. "Watch him," he added to Stoney, and hurried back into the house.

He tried to tamp down his suddenly crashing heartbeat. And the Texas-sized worry that went along with it. He assured himself that Webb couldn't have sneaked onto the ranch and gotten past the hands.

But he could have.

Webb could have done just that.

"Delaney?" Cash called out the moment he was inside. He figured that once he heard her voice or caught sight of her he could tell this bad gut feeling to take a hike.

That didn't happen.

Because he didn't hear her voice. Nor did Cash see her when he ran into the kitchen. She wasn't there, but his phone was lying on the floor.

And the back door was wide open.

A dozen possibilities went through his head.

None good. Delaney wouldn't have left unless something had gone horribly wrong. Or unless she'd been taken.

He scooped up his phone, shoving it into his pocket. His heartbeat revved up even more, and Cash drew his gun as he hurried to the back door. Holding his breath and praying, he peered out, bracing himself in case someone shot at him. Nothing. No gunfire. No Delaney. And there wasn't a ranch hand in sight.

His gaze darted around the grounds, and he spotted some smoke. Two ranch hands, Buck and Ted, were using feed sacks to beat down a small fire. Since the ground wasn't dry and that wasn't a spot where one of his workers would use open flames, Cash figured someone had set it. Probably to draw the attention of the ranch hands. Something it had succeeded in doing.

"Delaney?" he called out, knowing his shout would alert anyone waiting to attack him. But it also alerted the ranch hands.

"Everything okay, boss?" Stoney answered from the front of the house at the same time that Buck said, "Somebody dropped a cigarette butt on some hay. Don't worry. Me and Ted got it out."

Oh, but there was plenty of reason to worry, and it had nothing to do with a cigarette fire.

"Delaney's gone," Cash told them, and he hurried out into the yard. "Ted, get inside the house and search every inch of it. Buck, look in the barn to make sure she's not there."

Cash wanted to hold on to the idea that maybe something had spooked her, and she'd gone some place to hide. But she'd had his phone. If there'd been signs of trouble, she could have simply told Stoney, and he could have relayed that to Cash.

He fired more glances around and was gearing up to call out for her again when he spotted something. Movement in the grove of pecan trees on the east side of the ranch. The trees were tall and with plenty of low-hanging branches, giving someone lots of places to hide.

Cash headed in that direction.

"Delaney?" he shouted, and then he went with his gut. "Webb?"

And this time he got an answer. Someone fired a shot at him. It missed, smacking into the ground just to his right. Cash scrambled to the left, ducking behind a storage shed.

"Boss?" he heard Stoney yell.

"Call for backup," Cash shouted back. "I want deputies out here now. And don't let Ramone out of your sight," he added. "Webb's got Delaney."

Cash heard Ramone say something, but he tuned him out. He tuned out everything and pinpointed his focus to the pecan grove.

Glancing around the shed, Cash saw more movement, and while he couldn't make out Delaney and Webb, Cash was sure it was them. Since Delaney wasn't calling out for help, that meant Webb either had her gagged or was holding her at gunpoint. Maybe both.

Cash had to fight the urge to go running straight toward her. Had to fight the thought that Webb could and likely had already hurt her. Webb would enjoy hurting her, but obviously the man didn't want her dead yet or he would have killed her in the kitchen.

That didn't help the twisting and turning in his gut.

"Webb?" Cash yelled. "If this is a kidnapping, you've got demands. What are they?" He kept his voice all cop while he hurried to the other end of the shed where he hoped he'd have a better view.

And he did.

There, in the shadows of those branches, Cash could make out Delaney. She was standing in front of a man. Webb probably. Or rather she was forced to stand in front of him. Cash spotted the choke hold the man had around her neck. Along with the gun. He'd been right about Webb holding her at gunpoint.

Hell.

The fear scraped over him, flesh to bone, and in that instant Cash knew he'd do anything to save her. *Anything*. But to save her, he had to stay alive.

"Backup's on the way," Stoney shouted to him.

It wouldn't take long for his deputies to arrive. Less than twenty minutes. But that might be too much time if Webb had plans to take Delaney from here. The man must have had a vehicle. Or maybe he'd hitched a ride with his brother, who'd dropped him off at the end of the road. If so, if Ramone had a part in this, Cash would personally make sure he paid for what Webb was doing to Delaney.

"Well, Webb?" Cash tried again. "What are your demands?"

He didn't expect Webb to answer. But he did.

"I'm thinking it could be fun if Delaney watches her lover boy get gunned down," Webb said.

The man's tone was joking, but this wasn't anything to laugh at. Cash suspected that was exactly what Webb would try to do. Gun him down so that Delaney would have to see it.

Cash dropped down on his belly and started crawling. Thankfully, there were a lot of things between him and the pecan grove, and Cash used them for cover. First, some shrubs. Then an old watering trough.

"Well, Sheriff?" Webb mocked. "What do you think about dying today? Are you up for it?"

Cash didn't answer. He didn't want to give away his position as he moved as fast as he could, staying low and continuing to pray.

"Cat got your tongue?" Webb asked several moments later. "Oh, well. I wasn't in the mood for chitchat anyway. But I will give you a chance to say goodbye to Delaney. She's going with me right now before your deputies get here and try to mess with my fun."

Fun. Cash wished he could tear this sick SOB limb from limb. Webb wanted to hurt Delaney all because she hadn't kept his guilty butt out of jail.

Cash levered up a little once he reached the edge of the pasture fence. He got a better view of Delaney. At her face. He expected to see sheer terror there, but he saw the anger, too. And the determination that she was not going to let Webb take her without a fight.

He watched as she slammed her elbow into Webb's stomach. Webb cursed her, grunted and fired a shot. Not at Delaney. But at the shed. Maybe because he thought Cash was still there.

Delaney's expression turned to pain, no doubt from the gunshot blast so close to her ear. Cash knew from experience that it would make her temporarily deaf and might even cause some permanent damage.

That didn't tamp down Cash's temper any, but it made him realize he couldn't wait another second. Because Webb might forgo having his fun and turn the next shot on Delaney. Webb might not put up with her attempts to resist the abduction.

Cursing and tightening his choke hold on Delaney, Webb turned, heading in the direction of a trail that led out to the road. The moment he had his back turned, Cash made his move.

And he moved fast.

He ran hard, eating up the distance between Webb and him. Webb must have heard it, too, because the man whirled around, already bringing up his gun to take aim at Cash.

But Cash was just a second faster.

Cash tossed his own weapon aside, and in the same motion, he latched on to Webb's right wrist. He wrenched Webb's hand up so that the shot he fired went into the air. Cash elbowed Delaney to the side, getting her out of the way in case Webb managed to get off another shot.

Webb cursed again, the words vile and filled with rage. Cash didn't bother with his own curse words. He had one goal. Just one. To stop Delaney from being killed. With as much momentum as he could manage, Cash rammed his body into Webb's.

And he knocked Webb to the ground.

DELANEY DIDN'T HAVE time to react. Didn't have time to stop Webb or try to break her fall. She fell, hard, her head smacking against one of the trees. She was already in pain from Webb's choke hold and the gun blast, and the impact only added to it. Still, she'd take the pain because it meant she was alive.

But maybe not for long.

The fear hit her heavy in the chest. In the heart. Because the fear wasn't for herself but for Cash.

He'd seemingly come out of nowhere, and in a blur of motion, she had seen him drag Webb to the ground. Where they still were. Even though her vision was spotty, she could hear the sounds of the struggle. Fist against flesh. And she wasn't sure who was winning. Webb was not only a lot bigger than Cash, he had perhaps managed to hang on to his gun in the fall.

"Cash?" someone shouted, and she thought it was Ted, one of his ranch hands. "Are you okay?"

She wanted to know the same thing, and Delaney forced herself to get to her feet. It wasn't easy to do. Her head was spinning and everything seemed out of focus, as if her vision had been smeared with oil. Still, she could see Webb and Cash. Could see the life-and-death struggle that was going on.

Cash had both his hands clamped around Webb's right wrist. She'd been right about Webb hanging on to his gun. He had it, his finger poised on the trigger, and Cash was using all his strength to stop Webb from taking aim at her.

And Webb was making him pay for it.

Webb was pounding his left fist into Cash's side, obviously trying to break Cash's grip so he could try to kill them. Delaney had no intention of letting Cash fight this battle alone.

She glanced around, looking for something she could use to stop Webb, and she spotted Cash's gun on the ground. She scrambled to it, scooped it up. And took aim. Except she immediately realized she couldn't risk firing a shot. Not with Cash and Webb moving around. Any shot she fired now could hit Cash.

She caught some movement from the corner of her eye, and Delaney shifted toward it in case this was Ramone or someone else coming to help Webb. But it was the ranch hand, Buck. He had obviously run there because he was out of breath. He was also armed, and like Delaney he took aim, but he didn't have any better chance of a shot than she did.

Since she couldn't shoot, Delaney went after Webb's arm and the fist he was using to pummel Cash. She kicked Webb, causing him to howl in pain. He shifted but so did she, and she just kept kicking and stomping on any part of him she could reach.

The sound of the blast stopped her.

Webb had pulled the trigger.

Delaney's heart crashed against her ribs, and her breath stalled in her throat. *No.* Cash couldn't be shot. He couldn't be hurt. Or worse.

Yelling, and letting the rage ram through her, she stooped lower, and she saw the blood. It was on both Cash and Webb, so she couldn't tell which one of them had been hit.

Delaney clawed at Webb and scored his face with her nails before she took hold of his gun. He still had a fierce grip on it, but she couldn't let him get off another shot. Cash must've had the same plan, because he rammed his forearm into Webb's jaw and nose. More blood flew, and Delaney had the satisfaction of hearing the cartilage crunch from Webb's broken nose.

Webb called her a vicious name and reached out, trying to grab hold of her throat. Cash stopped him.

Grunting from the exertion, Cash twisted Webb around, slamming him back onto the ground. Buck rushed forward to stomp his boot onto Webb's right hand, and Delaney kicked aside Webb's gun.

In the back of her mind, it registered that she'd just disarmed a killer. A killer who wanted Cash and her dead. But she felt no relief whatsoever. Because the damage had already been done.

There was so much blood.

While Buck kept Webb pinned in place, Delaney had her first real look at Cash. And her heart dropped. A lot of that blood was on the front of his shirt. Soaked through to the skin.

"I wasn't shot," Cash blurted out.

She shook her head and lifted her gaze to his face. She could feel every muscle in her body trembling.

"I wasn't shot," he repeated. "Most of the blood is Webb's."

Delaney shifted her attention to Webb, who was now on his back. His breathing was labored, and he had almost no color in his face. However, there was plenty of color on his shirt, and Delaney could see that Cash was right. Most of the blood was indeed Webb's. She wasn't sure how it'd happened, but the bullet Webb had fired hadn't hit Cash.

It had hit Webb.

Now the relief came, and even though she didn't want to take her eyes off Webb, she threw her arms around Cash. She thought that maybe he needed that as much as she had. But it didn't last.

At the sound of approaching footsteps, they both whirled around. Cash snatched his gun from her and took aim. Her body braced for a fight, but bracing wasn't necessary because it was Jesse, Cash's deputy.

"Are you okay?" Jesse asked, glancing at Cash, Buck and her.

She was far from being okay. Delaney figured she was probably in shock, and her ears were still throbbing in pain, but at least they weren't seriously hurt. Well, Webb was, but her pity meter for him was below zero.

Cash turned to her and gave her a quick once-over, no doubt to verify that she hadn't been injured. She did the same to him. Or rather she tried. But it turned her stomach to see that blood all over the front of his shirt. Blood that could have been his if Webb had managed to turn the gun on him.

"I'm the one who needs help," Webb complained. "If you let me keep bleeding out, I'm gonna sue your butt." He added a sick, hollow laugh. One that made Delaney glad that she'd kicked him and broken his nose.

"Call for an ambulance," Cash told Jesse. "And then check to make sure Ramone hasn't gone anywhere. I want a deputy on him ASAP because he and I are going to have a conversation."

Delaney wanted in on that talk, too. It was entirely possible that Ramone had been a decoy, and that his visit was meant to be a distraction to draw Cash out of the house so that Webb could break in through the back door. The same way he'd gotten to Melanie. If Ramone had helped with either of the break-ins, then Delaney wanted him arrested.

"You think he'll live?" Buck asked, staring down at Webb.

"Hard to say," Cash muttered, and he used the pair of plastic cuffs that Jesse handed him to restrain Webb's wrists.

"You think I'm gonna get up and run when I'm bleeding like a stuck pig?" Webb snarled, and he laughed again. This time, though, he also coughed, and his color was definitely draining.

Delaney had never seen anyone die, but she thought that might change. Still, Cash tried to staunch the flow of blood by pressing his hands to Webb's chest. It didn't seem to help.

"Care to make a deathbed confession?" Cash asked him.

There was blood on his teeth when Webb grinned. "I haven't done anything wrong. I'm an innocent man."

That gave Delaney a whole new jolt of anger. She leaned over him, glaring right into his eyes. "You just tried to kill Cash, and you dragged me out of his house at gunpoint. You kidnapped and beat Melanie. And you blew up my house, nearly killing Cash and me in the process."

Webb met her eye to eye. "Now, you see, sweetheart, that's only partly true." He stopped, coughed, then grimaced. The pain was etched all over his face. "Care to guess which part is a big fat lie?" Even now, there was a taunt in his voice.

A taunt that gave her already raw nerves another jab. "All of it's true," Delaney insisted, and she prayed that it was.

Because if Webb had committed all those crimes, then it meant this was over. No more looking over her shoulder. No more danger.

Webb's next laugh was weak and filled with his hoarse breath. "No, sweetheart. You're wrong. I did try to kill you, and I'm the one who took Melanie. I dumped her by Jeb's house so I could mess with you and your lover boy's heads. But I didn't set that bomb. Not my style. I prefer, uh, hands-on. Plus, it would have been over way too fast. I like to take things slow when it comes to you."

The chill that came was winter-cold and rippled over her skin. "You set the bomb," she insisted.

Webb smiled that jeering smile, and even now, it packed a wallop. And so did what he said.

"Poor Delaney," Webb murmured. "Sweetheart, I'm not the only one who wants you dead."

Chapter Thirteen

Cash slipped his arm around Delaney's waist and got her moving away from Webb. There was no reason for her to stand there and let him continue to taunt her.

"Watch him," Cash instructed Jesse though he knew his deputy would do just that.

Webb might be hurt, was likely dying from the gunshot wound to the chest, but Cash didn't want the man to get a chance to do something else to harm Delaney.

"Oh, let her stay and listen," Webb joked. His voice was thankfully weaker now, and once Cash had gotten Delaney a few yards away, he could no longer hear Webb at all.

"Webb's lying," Delaney muttered. "He has to be lying. He was the one who put that bomb in my house."

Maybe. It would be just like Webb to lie about something that would cause the worry to eat away

at Delaney. And that was exactly what his words
would do.

*Poor Delaney. Sweetheart, I'm not the only one
who wants you dead.*

Because that might be true. There was Byers to
consider, and her father, too. Maybe Gil didn't actually want her dead, but if he'd set that bomb, then
he could do something else reckless that would get
her killed.

Byers was a different kettle of fish, however. He
might indeed actually want to kill Delaney, and that
was why Cash needed that interview with him. Unfortunately, Delaney might not be up for the trip.
She was trembling, and the adrenaline crash would
soon leave her spent. Along with that, she had a new
set of nightmares to deal with now that Webb had
come so close to killing her.

If Webb wasn't working alone, however, if someone else did indeed want "poor Delaney" dead, then
Gil and Byers weren't the only ones on Cash's suspect list. Right now, his top suspect was in his front
yard, and Cash didn't have to wait to talk to him.
He spotted Stoney holding Ramone at gunpoint.

"What happened?" Ramone called out. "Is that
really Webb back there?"

Cash ignored him, for the moment anyway, but
it seemed there was genuine surprise and worry in
his voice. Of course, those were emotions that could
be faked, and Cash wasn't ready to believe that it

was a coincidence that both Ramone and Webb had showed up at his ranch around the same time.

Nope, he wasn't buying that one little bit.

But he also wasn't going to put Delaney at risk. Just in case Webb had told the truth about someone else wanting her dead. That someone else could be Ramone, and it didn't matter that he was being held at gunpoint, because he could have hired a sniper to try to finish the job his brother had started. That was why Cash took Delaney back into the house.

He led her through the kitchen, hoping that just the sight of the scene wouldn't trigger flashbacks of her abduction. Cash moved fast, keeping hold of her hand, and he took her to the front door.

"Nobody's inside the house," Ted said. "I searched the place." He was in the doorway and also had a gun aimed at Ramone.

"Good," Cash said, adding a mumbled thanks. "I need you to go to the pecan grove and see if Jesse needs any help. More deputies and the ambulance will be here soon."

In fact, it would be a different kind of chaos in just a matter of minutes. His ranch was now essentially a crime scene with one man injured and another about to be interrogated.

"Stay behind me," Cash instructed Delaney. He moved into the doorway after Ted left.

Ramone's eyes widened when he saw Cash. Or rather when he saw Cash's blood-soaked shirt. "You're hurt?" Ramone asked. "Did Webb do that?"

"The blood is your brother's," Cash said, and he didn't bother to cushion the news because he needed to see his reaction.

Again, Ramone's surprise seemed like the real deal. Then again, he'd been standing out here a while where he'd had plenty of time to rehearse his responses. A rehearsal that Ramone would know was critical if he didn't want to be charged as an accessory to the dangerous stunt his brother had just tried to pull off.

"Webb's dead?" Ramone asked, and he swallowed hard.

"He's shot," Cash corrected, keeping the hard edge to his voice. He knew his eyes and expression were all cop. "Not sure if he'll make it."

Again, he watched for a reaction. This time, Ramone closed his eyes for a moment and muttered something under his breath that Cash didn't catch.

"Want to tell me what part you had in Webb's plan to kidnap and murder Delaney?" Cash demanded. "Or was it your plan and you brought Webb here to carry it out?"

Ramone was shaking his head before Cash even finished. Frantically shaking it. "I didn't know Webb was here, and I damn sure didn't have anything to do with his plan. I've got no beef against Delaney."

"But you knew that Webb was here to take her?" Cash argued.

"No." Ramone's answer was fast and practically

a shout. "I wouldn't do that. If I'd known he was going to hurt her, I would have found a way to stop him. I wouldn't have helped him. You have to believe me."

Cash didn't have to believe anything right now. Delaney had just been put through hell and back, and someone would pay for that. Webb, definitely. But maybe Ramone, too.

"I swear, I didn't know Webb was going to do this," Ramone went on. In the distance, there was the howl of sirens. "He called and asked me for money and a vehicle. That's it. I didn't even know he was in the area."

"And when's the last time you saw Webb?" Cash threw out there, hoping to get Ramone to slip up and admit that he had indeed been in contact with his brother.

But Ramone only shook his head again. "It's been months. I went to see him in prison, but that was around Christmas. I haven't seen him since."

Cash intended to push to find out if that was true. Maybe the security cams at the back of his ranch had picked up something. Like Webb's arrival shortly before Ramone's visit to tell Cash about his brother's demands for money and a vehicle.

The sirens got louder, and several moments later, an ambulance and a cruiser pulled into Cash's driveway.

"That way," Cash directed the EMTs when they hurried out. He motioned toward the pecan grove.

"A man's down. Gunshot wound to the chest. He's a dangerous fugitive and will stay restrained. Jesse will go with you in the ambulance."

As expected, no one gave him any flak about that, and he turned to the three deputies who stepped from the cruiser. Clark Whitlow, Dave Garcia and Marcella Hendrick. All three drew their weapons.

"Clark and Marcella, I need you to take him to the sheriff's office," Cash instructed, tipping his head to Ramone.

"But I didn't do anything," Ramone snapped. "I had no part in what my brother did."

"You need to be interviewed," Cash insisted. "It's procedure."

Obviously not pleased about that, Ramone shot him a glare. "I came here to help, not to be arrested."

"You're not under arrest," Cash assured him. Not yet anyway. "But if I find out you helped Webb, you will be."

That intensified Ramone's scowl, and Cash heard the man curse him as the two deputies led him to the cruiser.

With that ball rolling, Cash turned to Dave, the remaining deputy. "Jesse will go with Webb in the ambulance, so I need you to secure the crime scene. I need to stay with Delaney for now, and I don't want her anywhere outside. Not until we're sure Webb doesn't have any hired help."

Dave nodded, his gaze drifting to the cruiser as

it drove away. "What about Webb's brother? Did he *help*?"

"To be determined. For now, go to Jesse, and call me if Webb has said anything that isn't a lie or a taunt."

Of course, Dave might have trouble distinguishing a lie from the truth, but if there was anything questionable, his deputy would relay it to him. And he'd do that over the phone. That was one call that Cash wouldn't be putting on speaker. No need for Delaney to hear any more of Webb's garbage.

With his deputies on their way, Cash stepped back inside, shut the door and armed the security system. He'd have to disengage it if Dave, Jesse or the EMTs came to the house, but for now, he wanted the extra precaution. If there was truly a hired thug out there, Cash doubted the guy would try to break in, but then he'd never thought Webb would try it, either. Better to be safe than sorry.

And he was plenty sorry.

He'd left Delaney alone while he'd gone out and talked to Ramone. Alone and unsuspecting that Webb would get in and take her. He should have set the security system then. Or better yet, he should have demanded that Ramone go to the sheriff's office and report the call he'd said Webb had made to him. He damn sure shouldn't have put Delaney in a position where she could have been hurt or killed.

"You're beating yourself up," she said, reading

his thoughts. She touched his arm, rubbed lightly. "Don't."

"I should have done more to protect you." He groaned and started to scrub his hand over his face. That was when he realized he still had Webb's blood on him. Not just on his hands but on both his shirt and jeans.

Cash grumbled some profanity. "I need to bag my clothes. You, too. They probably won't be needed since I caught Webb in the act of committing a kidnapping, but it's procedure."

She nodded, sighed. The kind of sigh that let him know Delaney was starting to see the big picture. Webb might be in custody, but what had gone on here this morning would need to be investigated.

"Leigh sent over another pair of jeans and a top," she said, heading toward the guest room.

Cash followed her, not with plans to stand around gawking at her while she undressed, but because he didn't want her alone. Unfortunately, some gawking might happen. It was hard to convince his eyes, and other parts of him, that Delaney was hands-off.

He was about to tell her that he wanted her with him when he changed, but his phone rang. Delaney was in the process of unbuttoning her shirt, but she froze. Judging from her suddenly stark expression, she was expecting bad news.

And it might be.

That would fall into the "to be determined" category, too, because it was her father.

"Gil," Cash said, putting the call on speaker. He hoped that didn't turn out to be a mistake and that Gil wouldn't say something that would only add to the shell-shocked look in Delaney's eyes.

"I need to talk to Delaney," Gil insisted.

"Where are you?" Cash countered before Delaney could say anything.

"That's none of your business."

"Well, you see, it is," Cash assured him. "I've got a badge, remember, and I need to question you about a few things."

There was a long silence. "I need to speak to my daughter," Gil finally said, and there was nothing friendly about his tone.

Delaney didn't speak until Cash gave her a nod, and then she repeated Cash's question. "Where are you? And don't you dare say it's none of my business." Some of her shock had vanished, and her voice was a snarl.

"I'm safe," Gil told her after another long pause.

"I hired a bodyguard to protect you, and you snuck out of the house. Where are you?" Delaney didn't shout that last part, but it was close.

"A friend lent me his truck, and I'm driving around." There was nothing friendly or pleasant about his response. "And for the record, I didn't ask for a bodyguard and don't want one. In fact, I don't want you butting into my life. Just leave me the hell alone."

Delaney pulled back her shoulders. "Have you been drinking?" she came out and asked.

"I'm not going to discuss that with you." But his words were slurred just enough to make Cash believe the answer to that was yes.

Delaney sighed, shook her head. "Then tell me if you had anything to do with that bomb in my house."

Cash expected a fast denial from Gil. One filled with rage. But that didn't happen.

"I can see where your loyalties lie," Gil said, his voice practically a whisper now. "Cash has turned you against me."

"He hasn't," Delaney assured him. "But I want you to answer the question. Did you have anything to do with that bomb?"

However, she was talking to the air because Gil had already ended the call.

Cash quickly contacted dispatch to see if they could trace the call, but he figured Gil had made sure that wouldn't happen by using a burner. Still, they might get lucky. Maybe their luck would extend to Gil not hurting anyone if he truly was drinking and driving.

The moment he'd finished with dispatch, Cash's phone rang again. This time it was Jesse, and he answered it right away. He didn't put it on speaker, but Delaney was plenty close enough that she'd likely hear anyway.

"I'm in the ambulance," Jesse said, "but there's no hurry for us to get to the hospital. Webb just took the last breath he'll ever take."

WEBB WAS DEAD.

It had been several hours since Jesse had told them the news. Two hours for it to sink in that she no longer had to worry about a man who'd terrorized her, gone after people she cared about and had then tried to kill Cash and her.

Webb was dead.

Delaney kept repeating those words to herself in the hope that her body would finally believe it and would start settling down. Everything inside her still felt revved and raw. Every one of her nerves was much too close to the surface, putting her senses on hyperdrive. That was why she gasped when Cash came into the guest room, where she'd been pacing.

Her reaction caused him to sigh, and slipping his phone into his pocket, he went to her and pulled her into his arms. Something he'd been doing a lot since he'd rescued her from Webb. The close contact helped, but she had to wonder just how long it would be before she stopped feeling on edge. Maybe not until she knew for certain that Webb had been lying.

I'm not the only one who wants you dead.

That had to be a lie. It just had to be. Because if it wasn't, she might never have any peace.

She eased back just enough to look up at Cash

and study his eyes. Even though it wasn't anywhere near bedtime, he looked exhausted. Probably felt it, too. But at least he was no longer wearing clothes soaked with Webb's blood, and he smelled like the fresh soap from his shower rather than the scents from the fight.

Jesse had picked up their clothes and bagged them in case they were needed. The deputy had also brought Delaney several loaner outfits and had taken their statements. As part of procedure, Cash put himself on administrative leave. It was just a formality. No one believed he'd murdered Webb in cold blood, but until all the reports were filed, Cash wouldn't be able to do anything official.

Including interview Byers.

That had been moved to the following morning, and while Cash and she would be able to listen in, Jesse would actually be doing it. That would give the deputy time to get the report from Curley on Byers's medication, something that Jesse could maybe use to get Byers to confess that he'd tampered with her meds.

If he had actually done it, that is.

Delaney hadn't specifically asked Webb if he'd switched the medications, and she wished she had. Webb might have lied and said no, but it was just as possible that he would have admitted to it.

"I had the doctor drop off a sedative," Cash said. "I didn't figure you'd take it," he added when she started shaking her head, "but I wanted you to have the option. I doubt you'll get much sleep without it."

No, she wouldn't get sleep, and she might even consider taking it if she thought it would keep the nightmares at bay. But she doubted anything could do that.

"I'll be okay," she said. Which was a lie on so many levels.

There'd be nightmares even if she was awake. Her father was out there somewhere maybe doing harm to himself or someone else if he was driving around drunk. And she couldn't push aside that Cash had come so close to dying today.

"If Webb's gun had shifted—" she muttered. But she didn't get a chance to finish because Cash lowered his head and kissed her.

That was yet something else he'd been doing a lot since the fight in the pecan orchard. He'd been kissing her so that she wouldn't have the flashbacks. And it worked. For the moments when his mouth was on hers, Delaney was able to push everything aside and feel something good. Cash's kisses definitely qualified as good.

Then he eased back, studying her. "That put a little color back in your cheeks," he said.

The corner of his mouth hitched into a smile. A smile that didn't quite make it to his eyes. Probably because his thoughts were along the same lines as hers. After all, she'd come close to dying today, too.

"I don't want to think about what would have

happened if you hadn't gotten to me in time," she whispered.

Again, he stopped her with a kiss. But this one was different. It didn't have the feel of a gesture of comfort. There was some heat to it, and only got hotter when Cash deepened it.

Delaney felt the need start to slide through her, and mercy, it was good. The opposite of what she'd been feeling for the past couple of hours. Cash had always had a way of doing that, turning things around for the better, and he was definitely doing that now.

He lowered his hand to her back, nudging her closer until they were body to body. The kiss continued, meshing with that extra punch of having her breasts against his chest. It caused the heat to leap up even more, surrounding her so that this time when Cash started to move away, Delaney was the one who pulled him back to her. This time, she was the one who deepened the kiss.

Oh, his taste was so familiar. Like a soothing balm on the pain and fear. He could make that all go away. Make her just focus on one thing.

Him.

He made a sound, a groan that came from deep within his chest, and he broke the kiss. "You're not up to doing this," he said.

"I certainly feel up to it." And to prove it, she gave his midsection a bump with hers. But then she stopped when it occurred to her that they might not have time to land in bed. "Your deputies are still here?"

He shook his head. "The hands are patrolling the grounds, but I sent the deputies back to work."

So that meant no one would likely come to the door. If there were signs of trouble, one of his ranch hands would call him.

"With Byers's interview rescheduled, we don't have to go anywhere until morning," she reminded him. "I'd rather have you than a sedative."

She could see the quick debate in his eyes. The heat, too. He probably didn't want to lose focus by hauling her off to bed, but if so, that was a fight he lost because he kissed her again. And this kiss jumped straight to foreplay.

This time it was Delaney who made a sound. A purr of pleasure vibrated through her, and she melted against Cash. He took full advantage of the melting by moving that wildfire kiss to her neck. She felt so many things when he kissed her. The need. The ache for him. And the love. That was always there, too, and it was probably the reason she hooked her arm around his neck and started backing him toward the bed.

Cash moved with her, but he didn't let up on the kisses. Thank goodness. He went lower, kissing the bare skin of her throat and chest that the vee of her borrowed shirt exposed. He certainly started some fires there as well, and then spread even more when he touched her.

He moved his hand between their bodies. Cupping her right breast and swiping his thumb over her nipple. That caused her to purr again. And moan. She thought it wouldn't be long before she started to beg.

They fell back onto the bed, and in the same motion, Cash went after her shirt. His fingers worked fast to open the buttons, and he had it off her in no time.

The kisses started up again.

His mouth and tongue on her stomach, while he unhooked her bra. Once he'd freed her breasts, he kissed her there, too.

Her mind blurred from the heat, and Delaney savored the delicious feel of him taking her to the only place she wanted to go. But she didn't want to do this particular trip alone. Nope. Cash was going to be with her, and that meant getting him out of his clothes.

It wasn't easy to undress him. Mainly because Cash was doing the same thing to her, along with kissing every inch of her that his mouth encountered. He shimmied off her jeans, then her panties, and all while he was still fully dressed.

Delaney went white hot when he dropped some of those kisses between her legs, and she knew if she didn't do something fast, this would be over way too soon for her.

Again, she didn't want this to be solo, so she went after his shirt with a vengeance. It wasn't easy to get him out of his shirt, but it was so worth the effort to get her hands, and her mouth, on his bare chest. Kissing him like this brought back so many memories. Good ones. And for a little while, they could push aside all the bad things that had happened.

He grunted with pleasure when Delaney tackled his belt and zipper, but when she pushed his jeans off his hips, he stopped her.

"Condom," he growled.

For one heart-stopping moment she thought he was calling this off, that he was going to push her away. But instead he fumbled in his back pocket, located his wallet and got a condom. She remembered he always carried one there and was thankful for it. She didn't want to postpone this. She wanted Cash now.

Now happened as soon as he'd gotten the condom on. As if starved for her, he kneed her legs apart and pushed into her. Delaney had to fight hard not to climax right then and there. This was pleasure in its purest form. This was the kind of heat that continued to flame higher and higher with each stroke Cash made inside her.

Those strokes came harder, faster, deeper. Until Delaney could no longer hang on. Until her body gave way and tossed her over the edge.

Cash was right there, taking that plunge with her.

Chapter Fourteen

Cash scowled at the text he'd just gotten from Jesse.

We need to talk about Byers and Ramone.

Hell. That couldn't be good. Especially since it was nearly 9:00 p.m., which meant Jesse should have been off shift.

Cash eased out of bed, pulling on his jeans and shirt but not bothering to button or zip them. Moving as quietly as he could, he stepped out of the guest room so he wouldn't wake Delaney when he called his deputy. She was sleeping—peacefully, from the looks of it—and Cash wanted her to stay that way.

The fact that she hadn't even stirred with the ding of the text told him that she was well past being exhausted. He probably was, too, but apparently sex with Delaney worked better than a good night's sleep and a handful of energy pills. He was both revved and sated.

And worried.

Worried about Delaney's safety. About her father. About their future. Heck, they might not even have a future. That was a worry, too. But for now, Cash put all of that on the back burner and went into the kitchen to make the call to Jesse.

"How bad is the news?" Cash asked his deputy the moment Jesse answered.

"Well, it's not good," Jesse began. "Byers is refusing to come in for his interview, and he left you a message through his attorney. If you want to question him, then issue a warrant for his arrest."

Cash groaned. He hadn't wanted to go this route, especially because everything he had against Byers was circumstantial, but a warrant would compel the man to come in, and one way or another he needed to be interviewed. That connection he had with the meds Delaney had been given had to be addressed.

"His lawyer told me that he'd advised Byers to come in and clear up this matter," Jesse went on. "But Byers is refusing."

That left Cash with no choice. "Issue a warrant. Have him come in midmorning tomorrow." By then, Cash could decide if it was safe enough to take Delaney with him or if they'd go with the plan of having Jesse do the interview.

"That should rile Byers even more than he already is," Jesse commented. "And speaking of riled, Ramone's madder than a hornet. He's threatening to sue us for harassment."

That wasn't a surprise. Cash had already had a conversation with Jesse shortly after he'd finished the interview with Ramone, and Jesse had told him then that Ramone had been none too happy about being "hauled in" and treated like a criminal. All while he was grieving the death of his brother.

Cash might actually have some sympathy for the man if he could confirm that Ramone had had no part in the things that Webb had done. According to his earlier conversation with Jesse, his deputy hadn't been able to make that confirmation. Now that some hours had passed, though, Cash had let all of this settle in his mind and had come up with some new conclusions. Ones that they could hopefully back up with evidence.

"What's your gut feel about Ramone?" Cash asked. "Did he help set up Delaney's kidnapping?"

"Still not sure," Jesse said, but then paused. "There's plenty of anger in that man. The kind of anger that seethes and twists. I pressed him about that anger being directed at Delaney, but he insisted that he has nothing against her. You're the one he's riled about."

Yeah, Cash had gotten that message loud and clear. However, that didn't mean Ramone wasn't hiding how he really felt about Delaney. Because admitting his hatred for her would go to motive.

Cash turned when he heard the footsteps, and a yawning Delaney stepped into the kitchen. Her hair was mussed, and she was wearing one of his

T-shirts, so big it practically swallowed her. Still, she managed to look amazing.

"Issue the warrant," Cash repeated to Jesse. "Then go home and get some sleep."

"Will do," Jesse assured him and ended the call.

Cash slipped his phone in his pocket and went to her. "Sorry, I didn't mean to wake you."

"It's okay. I feel more rested than I have in a long time." She came up on her toes and kissed him. She kept it light, then eased back to meet his eyes. "Please tell me you're not regretting that we had sex."

No regrets about that, but Cash didn't believe it had just been sex. That was where he had regrets. Because he wasn't sure Delaney and he could get past their troubles to have a life together. A life not filled with family drama.

Or danger.

Cash still wasn't sure Webb's death had put an end to that.

"No regrets," he said, and he pulled her back to him for another kiss. A much longer one that stirred the heat and made him ache for her all over again. The heat and ache came to an abrupt halt, though, when she stopped and looked up at him.

"Why do you need a warrant?" she asked. She kept her body pressed against his. Kept her mouth close enough that her breath hit against his lips.

"It's for Byers. Apparently, he doesn't want to come in for questioning."

That put some concern in her eyes, and Cash

cursed Byers for it. "It's the only way he'll come in, and he needs to be questioned about those meds."

She nodded, and more concern showed on her face. "When Webb said he wasn't the only one who wanted me dead, do you think he was talking about Byers?"

That was possible, but it wasn't what Cash said to Delaney. "Webb could have said that just to spook you. A way of getting in one last dig."

"It worked," she muttered.

Silently cursing because he knew that was true, Cash pulled her tighter into his arms, and he considered just scooping her up and hauling her back to bed. But The slash of headlights outside the front windows stopped him, and he automatically moved in front of Delaney.

Instead of leaving her in the kitchen—a mistake he'd made earlier—he took hold of her hand, hurrying to the guest room to get his weapon and holster. While he was pulling on his boots, his phone rang, and he saw Stoney's name on the screen. Cash knew that the hands had divvied up shifts for keeping watch of the house, and apparently Stoney was on guard duty.

"Who just drove up?" Cash asked.

"I'm going out to check on that now," Stoney assured him.

Before his ranch hand could say more, Cash heard the shout, and he knew who'd come to pay them a visit.

Gil.

"Delaney, I need to talk to you," Gil shouted. His words were slurred, and when Cash peered out the front window, he saw Delaney's father staggering toward the house.

"My dad," Delaney muttered, and this time the worry in her expression went up a huge notch. She didn't go for the door, something that Cash thought she might do. Instead, she watched from over his shoulder. "He's drunk."

Oh, yeah. Well, unless he was putting on an act, but if so, it was a darn good one. Gil stumbled and would have fallen on his face if Stoney hadn't caught him.

"Get off me," Gil grumbled, pushing at Stoney, but Gil's shove missed Stoney by a couple of inches.

"Delaney?" Gil continued to shout. "I need to see my daughter. You can't keep her from me."

Cash could indeed keep her away from him, but Delaney was worried about her father, and if she truly wanted to see him, Cash doubted he could talk her out of it.

"I have to tell Delaney goodbye," Gil yelled. "I need to tell her this is the last time she'll ever see me."

"Oh, mercy," Delaney muttered, and Cash heard her slow intake of breath. "He's going to try to kill himself again."

"Maybe," Cash conceded. But this could be some

kind of trick similar to what Webb had pulled when he'd sneaked into the house.

"Boss, what you want me to do with him?" Stoney asked, letting Gil fall to the ground. Groaning and cursing, Gil landed on his back.

Cash had a quick debate with himself and considered calling his night deputy to come out and take Gil into custody, but one look at Delaney, and he knew he had to do more than that.

"See if you can get him to the porch," Cash instructed, and he glanced at Delaney. "I'll let Gil in the house if that's what you want, but I'll search him for weapons and cuff him."

He figured Delaney would balk about the cuff, but after only a couple of seconds, she nodded. It made Cash wonder if she'd truly accepted that her father might have had a part in setting that bomb. Then again, maybe she was just at a point where she wasn't ready to trust anyone who could be a person of interest in this investigation.

Cash hurried to the closet and got a pair of plastic cuffs from a supply bag he kept there. He went back to the window and watched Stoney drag Gil to his feet. Not easily. Gil was a big man, and wobbling all over the place, but the ranch hand finally got Gil to the porch.

"Stay right behind me," Cash told Delaney.

She did exactly that as he used his phone to disarm the security system and open the door. Cash reached for Delaney's father, pulling the man inside.

Not just into the foyer but away from the door and into the living room. The first thing Cash smelled was the strong stench of alcohol. If Gil wasn't truly drunk, then he'd doused his clothes with what smelled like cheap whiskey.

With Stoney standing guard, Cash got Gil on the floor and frisked him. No weapon, other than a pocketknife that Cash tossed onto the coffee table.

"No need for this manhandling," Gil complained. He threw a punch at Cash. It missed him, but Gil knocked Cash's phone from his hand, and it skittered across the hardwood floor. "I just need to talk to my girl."

Ignoring Gil and the phone, Cash spun Delaney's father around and cuffed his hands behind his back. Once he was sure the man was secure, he looked at Stoney. "Shut and lock the front door. I need you to patrol the yard and make sure no one came here with our drunk visitor."

Stoney nodded and headed right out, doing as Cash had instructed. Since his phone was somewhere on the floor, Cash hurried to the foyer and used the keypad by the door to rearm the security system. He didn't want any repeats of what had happened with Webb.

"Give me one good reason why I shouldn't haul you off to jail," Cash snarled, coming back into the living room and standing over Gil.

Gil looked up at him and blinked hard as if trying to focus, when his attention landed on Delaney.

"My girl," the man said, and tears filled his eyes. "I'm sorry. So sorry."

"For what?" she asked, her voice trembling.

But Gil didn't get a chance to answer. The power went off, plunging the room, and the house, into total darkness.

DELANEY FROZE. HER BODY did, anyway. But the thoughts started to race through her head. Bad thoughts. And she automatically flashed back to the moment when Webb had grabbed her and put a gun to her head.

Was that about to happen now?

Had someone managed to get inside the house?

Worse, had her father arranged this drunken ruse so that someone could get in and kill Cash and her?

Delaney wanted to demand to know if Gil had indeed done something like that, but her instincts were telling her to stay quiet. If her father was in on this, he already knew her location in the room, but there was no reason to telegraph it to someone who'd come with him.

She went stiff when someone took hold of her arm, and Delaney started to fight back so that she wouldn't be kidnapped.

"It's me," Cash said.

He pulled her to his side, and she heard the slide of his gun against the leather of his holster when he drew his weapon. She also heard other sounds. Footsteps. Someone shuffling around, and she wished Cash had his phone so he could use the flashlight on it. The last she'd seen it, it was on the floor, and right now she couldn't see her hand in front of her face much less the floor.

Cash tensed when a low sounding beep began to pulse through the house. "It's the backup to the security system," he whispered.

She hoped that meant the alarm would sound if someone broke in, but Delaney knew it could mean something else.

Someone could have already gotten inside.

That sent her heart pounding, but she tried to tamp down the panic and fear. Neither emotion would do them any good right now.

With his left arm around her waist, Cash started to step back with her. Leading her to the corner of the living room, she realized. Away from the doors and windows.

Away from her father, too.

"What about Gil?" she asked, trying to keep her voice as soft as possible.

"He's staying quiet," was all Cash said.

Yes, he was quiet, and Delaney considered that he might have passed out. Well, if he was as truly drunk as he'd seemed, that was possible. But her father also might not want them to know where he was. Even though he was cuffed, that wouldn't stop him from getting to his feet and doing whatever it was he'd come here to do.

She thought of Cash's phone, of the way her father had knocked it from his hand. Had that been intentional? If so, it'd been a good move on his part because now Cash had no way to call for backup. He could shout for Stoney, who was almost certainly nearby, but a shout might come at a high price if it caused a killer to pinpoint their location and shoot them.

There were more sounds of movement, and as Delaney's eyes began to focus in the dark, she thought she saw a blur of motion. Cash must have seen something, too, because he turned his body, and she thought that maybe he shifted his gun in that direction.

Mercy. This couldn't be happening. Not again. And it was worse than when Webb had taken her out of the house and to the pecan grove. There'd been places outside for Cash to take cover, but right now both of them were exposed, especially if someone was wearing night vision goggles.

Cash put his mouth right against her ear. "I need to get my phone."

She nodded. Delaney thought it was somewhere by the living room chair that was close to the foyer. Obviously, Cash thought that, too, because he started to inch them in that direction, all while staying close to the wall.

"Duck down," he instructed when they reached a window.

Delaney did, and with the same snail's-crawl pace,

they moved to the other side. Then they repeated the maneuver as they got past the second window.

With each step, her eyes adjusted even more, and Delaney could see the shapes of the furniture and the arched entrance that separated the foyer from the living room. She glanced around on the floor, searching for both her father and Cash's phone.

She didn't see either.

Cash muttered some profanity, his voice hardly making a sound, but she clearly heard the frustration. They needed that phone.

With his arm still around her, Cash eased her down lower until they were in a crouch. Delaney could see more shapes and shadows, but there just wasn't enough moonlight filtering in through the windows for her to see anything on the dark hardwood floor.

"There's a flashlight in the kitchen," Cash murmured.

She remembered it being in the drawer next to the fridge. It wasn't far away, but with the darkness and the possible threat, it suddenly seemed miles away. They needed the light not only to find the phone but so she could also check on her father. Delaney wanted to see his face, and she thought that with just one look she might be able to tell if he'd had any part in all this.

Still crouching, Cash got them moving toward the kitchen, but they'd hardly made it a few inches when he cursed again. He let go of her so he could pick up something, and Delaney quickly realized it was the plastic cuffs. Maybe the ones that'd been on her father, but if so, they'd been cut.

That dropped her heart to her knees.

The odds were her father couldn't have cut them off himself. Which meant he'd had help. An accomplice. Or perhaps he was the accomplice here and had just helped someone get into the house. Someone who could try to kill Cash. Delaney didn't want to believe that her father would intentionally make her a target, but then she remembered what he'd said right before the electricity had gone off.

I'm sorry. So sorry.

She'd thought he was apologizing for being drunk and showing up at Cash's, but it could have been a whole lot more than that. He could have put something in place that could lead to her murder. Or rather her attempted murder. Because Delaney had no intention of just allowing someone to kill Cash and her. She'd fight and fight hard—even if it meant that fight was against her own father.

Cash tossed the cuffs aside and got them moving again. As they inched their way to the kitchen, Delaney listened. And kept watch. She no longer heard footsteps, and there were no more of those shuffling sounds. Sounds that had probably been someone cutting those restraints from her father's hands.

But where was her father now?

And better yet, who and where was the person who'd freed him?

Delaney braced herself in case Cash and she ran into that person. But they didn't. They made it all the way to the kitchen without her seeing or hearing anything.

When Cash reached the kitchen drawer, he fumbled inside and came up with a small flashlight. He passed it to her, no doubt so his hands would be free if he needed to shoot or fight.

"Go ahead and turn it on," Cash instructed. "But keep the light aimed at the floor."

Good idea. They might be able to use the light to find the phone before her father or someone else saw it and zoomed in on them. Of course, maybe the person had already done the zooming in. Maybe he was just waiting for a clean shot.

Even though her fingers were trembling, Delaney located the flashlight switch and turned it on. The light spilled over the kitchen floor, and that was when she saw something. Dark-colored drops on the white tile.

And she immediately knew what it was.

Blood.

Chapter Fifteen

Cash looked at the blood and cursed. Blood drops that led from the kitchen straight to the back door.

Hell.

This situation had gone from bad to worse because he figured that blood belonged to Delaney's father.

All those shuffling sounds and footsteps had probably been someone "helping" Gil get out of the house. Maybe Gil had been in on the plan. Maybe not. But even if Gil was hurt, it didn't mean he wasn't going to help someone else try to kill Delaney and him.

"My father," Delaney whispered, her breath rising. Cash could hear the panic in her voice.

Cash held her back. He certainly didn't want her rushing out into the backyard, where she could be gunned down. The killer might have counted on her doing just that, and perhaps that was why Gil's blood was on the floor.

"I need a phone," Cash muttered. He had to call

for backup. Maybe an ambulance, too, depending on how badly the bleeding person was hurt.

He glanced around, peering into the darkness, and didn't see anyone. Cash didn't hear anyone, either. That didn't mean someone wasn't inside. Still, he was armed and had a flashlight that he could use to locate his phone.

Maybe.

It was possible that Gil or the person who'd gotten him out of the house had also taken the phone. That way, it would buy these SOBs time to do whatever it was they planned to do. Obviously, it wasn't just to gun Delaney and him down, or that would have happened when the person got Gil out.

But Cash had to add another *maybe* to that theory.

Gil and his accomplice/abductor could have wanted to get Delaney's father out of the way before any shooting began. That way, Gil would either be protector or used as a pawn by having this attack pinned on him. That definitely wasn't a settling thought.

"Stay right next to me," Cash told Delaney.

She gave a shaky nod, dragged in an even shakier breath, and he hated that she was having to go through this all over again. This was worse than Webb grabbing her, because now she had the added worry about her father. Delaney had to know that he could be bleeding out right now.

Or Gil could already be dead.

If her father had helped orchestrate this ploy for

someone to get to her, then maybe his usefulness was over and done. His accomplice knew the only way to tie up a loose end was by killing Gil. But if so, why hadn't the person just murdered Gil in the living room? Why cut off his restraints and get him out?

Cash didn't know the answer to either of those questions, but he sure as hell hoped to find out soon.

In case someone was watching the house, Cash turned off the flashlight and got Delaney moving back toward the living room. However, they'd only made it a few steps when Cash heard something he definitely hadn't wanted to hear.

The slight creak of the front door opening.

He stopped, positioning himself in front of Delaney but also keeping his body at an angle so he could continue to watch the back door. He didn't want this to be another ruse where someone distracted them so that someone else could sneak in and attack them from behind.

Cash hoped the footsteps he heard in the foyer belonged to Stoney or one of his other ranch hands, but he didn't want to risk calling out to verify that. If he was wrong, it could get Delaney and him shot.

Without saying anything, Cash eased Delaney back so he could maneuver her to the side of the fridge. It wasn't bulletproof, but it was easy cover. It was also close enough to the back door in case they had to attempt a quick escape.

The footsteps stopped in the living room, and

Cash figured the person was doing the same thing he was. Listening. Maybe waiting, too, for Delaney and him to make the first move.

Cash tightened his grip on his gun and took aim as best he could, but he had no idea exactly where this "visitor" was. And he couldn't just blindly shoot, either, in case it was one of the ranch hands. So Cash stood there, his heart pounding, and the adrenaline surging through him. Preparing him for the fight. Except Cash didn't want a fight, not with Delaney right next to him.

No.

He wanted to take out this killer when he was sure Delaney was safe. Unfortunately, Cash had no idea when that would be.

Cash detected some movement. Not footsteps. But something else. And a few seconds later, he realized exactly what that *something* was. Movement from someone who was trying to kill them.

A gunshot slammed into the fridge just on the other side of where Delaney and he were standing.

Cursing, Cash automatically pushed Delaney down, and it wasn't a second too soon. Another shot came, and this one tore through the fridge as if it were paper. The bullet exited and penetrated the wall and went into the pantry.

Cash wanted to return fire. To stop this SOB in his tracks. But to shoot, he'd have to leave cover. Where he'd be an easy target. If he got killed, Delaney would be a sitting duck.

Cash had a quick debate as to what to do, and he decided it was too risky to stand their ground. Obviously, the shooter had an idea of where they were. Maybe because he was using night vision. He could stand where he was and keep firing until he hit one or both of them.

"Stay low," Cash whispered to her, and he hoped she could hear him over the sound of the third blast.

He didn't waste any time. With them in a crouch, Cash got Delaney to the back door. He eased it open, looked around. And prayed. He didn't see anyone, but of course, a second gunman could be out there, waiting for them to do exactly what Cash was about to do.

"Move to the right side of the porch," Cash added to her.

The moment Delaney and he were outside, he picked up the pace and got them moving as fast as he could to the porch swing. Again, it was lousy cover, but if the gunman came onto the back porch, Cash would have a shot—especially since the moonlight made it easier for him to see. Plus, Delaney and he could drop down into the yard if things took a bad turn.

Things did indeed take a bad turn when Cash saw more dark-colored drops on the porch. More blood. He was sure of it. And these drops led off the porch and into the backyard.

The fear crawled through him when he heard Delaney gasp, and for one heart-stopping moment he thought someone was about to grab her. Or worse. That someone was about to shoot her. But when he followed her pointing finger to the yard, Cash saw the reason for the gasp.

Someone was lying facedown on the grass, only a few yards from the shed.

It was a man, and Cash was pretty sure that was blood he saw on the back of the guy's shirt.

"My father," she whispered.

While he kept an eye on the back door, Cash leaned a little so he could get a better look at the man. And his chest tightened, vising his ribs until he thought they might crack. Because it wasn't Gil.

It was Stoney.

Hell. His ranch hand was down.

Cash wondered if the blood in the kitchen and on the porch could be Stoney's. He wasn't moving, and with all that blood, he could be dead. Cash hadn't heard a gunshot in the backyard, but that didn't mean someone hadn't fired using a silencer. Of course, there were plenty of other ways to kill, and it was possible that Stoney had been stabbed.

Delaney made a soft gasp when there was some movement in the kitchen, and Cash volleyed his attention between the yard and the door. That was because the person in the kitchen could be a decoy or something. Someone meant to distract them so the killer could come at them from somewhere on the grounds.

Cash cursed himself for not grabbing a knife

from the kitchen. If he had thought of it, Delaney would have had a weapon in case it came down to a fight. However, he prayed that things wouldn't get that far. He took aim at the door, and if any one of their suspects came out, he'd be ready to put a stop to this.

The door creaked open just a couple of inches, and Cash dragged in his breath. Waiting. Listening. And steeling himself up to do whatever necessary to keep Delaney alive.

A hand jutted out from the opening, and in the blink of an eye, the person tossed something onto the porch. It thudded onto the wood planks and then rolled. It wasn't until it got closer to them that Cash realized what it was.

"A grenade," Cash spat out.

He didn't wait for Delaney to react. Hooking his arm around her waist, Cash tumbled off the porch with her. They landed hard on some rocks and shrubs, but he quickly pulled Delaney to her feet and got them running.

DELANEY HAD ONLY gotten a glimpse of the grenade that had been thrown out on the porch, but a glimpse had been more than enough to confirm that Cash and she were in huge trouble.

They couldn't stay there and wait to be blown to bits, but running out into the yard meant they could be gunned down.

Still, they ran.

Cash made sure of that. He kept a firm grip on her arm, and moving fast, they headed for the side of the barn. They nearly made it there, too, when the blast tore through the air.

Delaney staggered and risked looking back. The porch had been ripped apart, and bits of the wood and railing were flying across the yard.

Cash dragged her to the side of the barn, positioning them back-to-back and in a crouching position. "Keep watch. If you see anyone, let me know."

Delaney nodded, and with her breath gusting, she fired glances around, looking for the person who obviously wanted them dead. But she didn't see anyone. Well, no one other than Stoney, who was still facedown on the ground. Thankfully, the ranch hand was out of the way from the falling debris, so he likely wouldn't be hit. However, he also hadn't moved, which couldn't be a good sign.

Maybe because he was dead.

Delaney had to shove that possibility aside because it would scrape her nerves raw, and that wouldn't help anything. She needed to stay focused, alert. That was the only way they could stay alive.

As bad as the grenade had been, at least it would alert the ranch hands, and one of them would certainly call the cops and maybe even an ambulance. If they could make a call, that is. Delaney had a sickening thought, one that clawed its way up her throat. If the killer had murdered or injured Stoney, he might have done the same thing to the other ranch hands.

Oh, mercy.

There were three other hands somewhere on the grounds. Maybe even in the bunkhouse. They'd been vigilant, standing guard and patrolling the grounds, but that didn't mean someone couldn't have sneaked up on them one at a time.

Had her father done that?

Delaney still didn't want to believe he'd had any part in this, but she had to accept that he might have helped set it up. Maybe he'd done that without realizing what the would-be killer planned to do. Maybe her father had figured out that she was the target, and tried to fight back. That could explain the blood.

And maybe she was just hanging on to false hope.

Either way, she needed to find her father and discover if he was the reason this attack was happening. Of course, for her to get those answers, Delaney needed to find him alive.

She thought of the blood in the kitchen and on the porch. It wasn't a huge amount, so maybe he didn't have a life-threatening injury. Or maybe it wasn't his blood at all. That twisted away at her, too, but Delaney had to consider that her father might be the attacker here and that anyone in his path was a possible victim.

A second blast thundered through the silence, and Delaney could have sworn that it shook the ground beneath her. She didn't dare look back to see how much damage this one had caused. She kept her attention pinned to the back of the barn and the pasture that spread out behind it.

And then she saw it.

Some movement on the ground at the back of the barn. She pinned her gaze there and considered alerting Cash. But it could be nothing. And Delaney didn't want to pull his attention from the house, especially since that was where the grenades had come from. Their attacker could still be inside, but it was just as possible that he'd already gone out through the front door. If so, then Cash would be able to see if he came to the backyard to try to finish what he had started.

Delaney saw another flutter of movement by the barn, and she heard something. It sounded like moaning. The kind of moan a person would make if they were in pain.

"Someone's back there," she whispered to Cash.

Cash immediately spun around, pinning her against the barn. Using his body to shield hers. Delaney didn't want him doing that. Risking himself for her, but now was hardly the time to tell him that she couldn't lose him. She just couldn't.

There was another moan, this one louder than the first, and Delaney saw more movement. Because of the heavy shadows, she couldn't be certain, but she thought it was another man. Maybe one of the ranch hands.

Maybe her father.

She forced herself to stay put, and she tamped down her instincts to go to him. To make sure he was okay. She couldn't do that because it could be a trap.

That possibility tightened every muscle in her body, and she held her breath for so long that her lungs began to ache. Cash stayed in place, protecting her, while he volleyed glances between the house and the back of the barn where the person was still moaning.

Delaney focused straight ahead. At the shed. At Stoney. At the groves of trees that rimmed the pasture. There wasn't nearly enough light for her to see if anyone was lurking in those trees, but it would be a good spot for a sniper. Of course, a sniper might not be needed at all if the person who'd thrown those grenades got close enough to Cash and her to toss another one at them.

"I'm going to try to get us to the bunkhouse," Cash whispered.

That made sense, because even if the ranch hands were all down, there'd likely be a phone in the bunkhouse. Or other weapons they could use to defend themselves. But the bunkhouse was behind the barn, and there were plenty of places where they could be attacked along the way. Still, just sitting here wasn't a smart move. Another grenade could come their way at any second.

"Stay low and keep watch," Cash whispered to her. "I'll deal with whoever that is on the ground."

Delaney considered how that might play out. Perhaps with a gunfight. But then she heard something else. Something that sent an icy shock through her entire body.

The sound of dogs growling.

Chapter Sixteen

Cash had prayed things wouldn't get any worse. But the sound of those barking, snarling dogs meant that Delaney and he had to get out of there fast.

Judging from the sound of the barks, these were Ramone's Dobermans. Maybe the dogs had gotten loose again, but Cash thought it could be a lot more than that. Ramone could have set them loose as a way of finishing what he'd started by throwing those grenades at them.

"Let's go," Cash told Delaney, pulling her to her feet.

She'd already started moving toward the back of the barn, away from the dogs, but directly toward the man who was lying on the ground. There were barn doors at the rear that they could slip through and get away from the Dobermans, but first Cash had to deal with the guy on the ground. If it wasn't one of his ranch hands, then it was possibly someone involved in the plot to kill Delaney and him.

Behind them, Cash heard the dogs gaining

ground. They would no doubt attack, and that had Cash considering if he should make a stand and try to get them to back off. The problem with that was while he was dealing with the Dobermans, the person who wanted them dead could just pick off Delaney and him. In fact, the dogs could be a ruse making it easier for that to happen.

Cash kept them running until they reached the man, who was now trying to sit up. Not one of his hands.

But Gil.

Delaney's father was still moaning, and there was a cut on his head as if someone had clubbed him. The injury looked real. *Looked*. However, Cash figured it could be a clever fake and part of whatever this sick plan was that had already been set in motion.

"We can't leave him out here," Delaney insisted, already reaching down to take hold of her father's arm.

No, they couldn't, but that didn't mean Cash intended to trust the man. After all, if it hadn't been for Gil, Cash would have a phone and would have already called for backup.

Cash let go of Delaney so he could grab Gil. "If you try to hurt Delaney," he warned her father, "I'll kill you. Understand?"

Gil mumbled something that he didn't take the time to catch, but Cash kept his eye on their surroundings and then threw open the barn door and practically tossed Gil inside.

Just as the dogs reached them.

Cash felt the gut punch of fear that Delaney could be mauled to death, and he fired a shot over the dogs' heads. The sound of the blast stopped them long enough to shove into the barn. Together, they slammed the doors shut.

The dogs continued to bark and growl and began pawing at the door. Cash slid the board latch in place and whirled back around to make sure Gil wasn't about to attack them. The only light in the barn came from a battery-operated bug zapper, but it was enough for Cash to see Gil. He was still on the ground and wasn't making any attempt to get up.

Good. That was where Cash wanted him to stay.

Cash didn't have any cuffs with him, but he grabbed some hay baling twine and used it to tie Gil's hands. It might not hold, and it darn sure wouldn't prevent the man from trying to run, but at least Gil wouldn't be able to pick up something and try to bash them with it.

"Are you working with Ramone?" Cash asked him. "Did the two of you set all of this up?"

Gil moaned again and shook his head. "Set up what? What's going on?"

Cash wanted to know the same damn thing, but this wasn't the time to play twenty questions with Gil. He had to take some precautions and take them fast.

"This way," Cash said, and he caught on to Delaney's hand to lead her behind some stacked hay bales. It wasn't much cover, but it was better than nothing. "In case there's another grenade."

Even in the dim light, Cash could see the terror in Delaney's eyes. He cursed that terror. Cursed himself for not having kept her safe.

Delaney reached out for him when he started to move away and go back to Gil. "You should be behind cover, too," she pointed out, and her gaze flicked to her father. "Him, too. He can tell us who's trying to kill us."

Probably, but at this point having a name wasn't nearly as important as stopping the person. Still, Cash dragged Gil away from the barn door. But he put the man yards away from Delaney.

"Cash?" someone called out.

Ramone.

Cash was sure of it. He didn't respond, and he motioned for Delaney to stay quiet. Of course, it was possible that Ramone already knew they were in the barn, but in case he didn't, Cash didn't want to make this easy for him.

"Cash?" Ramone called out again. "Delaney? Are you all right? What the hell happened to your porch?"

The dogs stopped barking, and Cash could hear them running away from the barn. Probably heading toward their owner.

"Go get in the truck," Ramone said, and Cash hoped that meant he was calling off the dogs—literally. But if Ramone had been the one to set the Dobermans on them, why would he do that?

Maybe as part of the ploy to draw them out of the barn?

If so, Cash wasn't buying it. He shifted his attention to the front barn doors, took aim with his gun and waited.

"Cash, I got a call from one of your hands," Ramone shouted. "He didn't give me his name, but he said my dogs were over here and that I should come and get them right away. I'm really sorry. I don't know how they got out." He paused. "Are you two okay? Was there some kind of explosion in your kitchen?"

Ramone's concern sounded like the real deal, but Cash still didn't answer.

"I'm calling 911," Ramone finally said, and a few moments later, he cursed. "Hell, one of your ranch hands is on the ground."

There was the sound of running footsteps, and Cash grumbled some profanity. If Ramone was the killer, Cash couldn't just stand by while he murdered Stoney.

Cash snatched up a pitchfork and handed it to Delaney. "Use it if you need to," he told her.

Of course, that had to cause her fear to soar, but Delaney stood, gripping it like a weapon. She looked plenty ready to defend both of them if it came down to it.

Cash hurried to the front barn door, eased it open

and leaned out enough to take aim at Ramone. "Stop where you are," he warned Ramone.

Ramone whirled around, and he must have had no trouble seeing Cash's gun because he cursed and lifted his hands in the air. He had his phone in his right hand, but his left one was empty. No signs of a weapon. Of course, he could have one tucked in the back waist of his jeans.

"I don't know what you think I've done," Ramone snarled on a huff. "But the only reason I'm here is to get my dogs. I'm pretty sure someone let them out of their pen."

"And who would have done that?" Cash fired back.

"I don't know," Ramone repeated, tipping his head to Cash's house, "but I'm guessing it was the same person who did that to your porch." His forehead bunched up. "Are you and Delaney okay?"

Cash ignored that question and went with one of his own. "Did you call 911?"

"Not yet. You want me to do that now?"

"Why don't you toss me your phone, and I'll make the call?" Cash countered. That way, he'd be sure it would actually go through and not be part of Ramone's ruse to make Cash believe that help was on the way.

"Okay." Ramone's voice and expression were now all caution.

Or pretend caution anyway.

But with his left hand still in the air, Ramone

inched closer. Cash didn't plan on letting him get too close. When Ramone was a couple of yards away, he'd have him throw the phone toward him. If Ramone had had no part in this attack, then Cash could snatch up the cell and call for help. However, if Ramone was up to his eyeballs in this, then he'd likely use this latest incident with the dogs to get closer to Cash. Maybe so he could try to kill him. However, if he tried that, Cash would take him out.

Even though Cash didn't want to take his attention off Ramone, he glanced at the barn to make sure Delaney was okay. She was. For now, anyway. She still had hold of the pitchfork, and Gil hadn't moved an inch from where Cash had put him.

Ramone was still moving toward him when Cash heard the swooshing sound. Not a gunshot fired from a silencer. This was bigger than a handgun. And Cash quickly saw what it was.

Someone had launched another grenade.

And this one landed right next to Ramone's feet.

FROM THE MOMENT DELANEY had heard Ramone's voice, she'd suspected there'd be more trouble.

And there apparently was.

Ramone yelled out, "What the hell?" a split second before Cash ducked back into the barn.

Much to her shock, Ramone was right behind Cash, and Cash didn't stop him from bolting into the barn. The two men slammed the door shut and continued running to the side of the barn where she was. Both of them dived behind the hay bales with her, with Cash positioning himself between Ramone and her.

Before she could ask what was happening, Delaney heard the third explosion. This one was louder than the other, and it shook the barn, causing bits of hay and dust to spill down from the hayloft.

"He's playing with us," Cash growled. He gave her a quick glance as if to make sure she was okay, and then he shifted his attention to Ramone.

"Did you have anything to do with this?" Cash demanded.

"What the hell is *this*?" Ramone demanded right back, and even though Delaney couldn't see his expression, the man certainly sounded shocked and scared. "Was that really a grenade?"

"Yeah," Cash verified. "And if you helped set that up, then I swear that you'll pay hard for it."

"Set it up?" Ramone challenged. "I could have been killed, and I sure as heck didn't launch a grenade at myself. It landed right by my feet. If it'd gone off just a couple of seconds sooner, I'd be a dead man."

Since Cash didn't disagree with that, Delaney got a mental picture of what'd happened outside the barn. Ramone had called off the dogs, but while he'd been talking with Cash, someone had fired a grenade at him. Someone who wasn't her father. Wasn't Ramone.

And that left one person from their suspect list.

Byers.

"He wants us all in here," Cash said as if talking to himself. He cursed. "Call 911," he added to Ramone. "Ask for backup."

She heard Ramone punch in the numbers on his phone and then relay Cash's order and their situation. It wouldn't take long for the deputies to arrive, but if their attacker had more grenades, then he could toss one at the barn. That would only take a couple of seconds. And she doubted the barn was strong enough to withstand a direct blast.

"We have to get out of here," Cash muttered. "He plans to kill us all."

"He?" Ramone asked when he finished the call.

Cash didn't get a chance to answer, because someone called out to them.

"I'm betting you're all at each other's throats right about now," the man shouted. "I'm going to give it a minute or two and see if you off each other for me."

Byers. He was the one behind this. The one who'd been trying to kill Cash and her.

That realization slammed into her like a Mack truck. She'd been the one to invite Byers into their lives by hiring him. Of course, she hadn't asked for this, but if she'd never...

Delaney stopped the guilt trip and rethought everything. Fitting the pieces together like a puzzle.

"Byers set this up," she said.

"Yeah," Cash readily agreed. "And we have to

get out of here. Because I'm betting Byers has another grenade."

"Byers?" Ramone repeated, shaking his head. "Why the hell would he do something like this?"

Delaney intentionally answered in a loud enough voice for Byers to hear. "Byers wants to kill me because he thinks I got your brother a break when Webb wasn't convicted of first-degree murder."

"Webb got manslaughter," Byers snarled, confirming that he had indeed heard her. "Webb should have gotten the death penalty, and you managed to get him a slap on the wrist."

A twenty-year sentence wasn't exactly a slap on the wrist, but Byers wouldn't want to listen to that. Nor would he want to hear that there simply hadn't been enough evidence to prove premeditation for a first-degree murder conviction.

"A jury gave Webb that sentence," Cash pointed out.

"A jury that heard only what Delaney wanted them to hear. And don't tell me she was just doing her job. She made sure a killer would get out of jail so he could kill again. Too bad Webb didn't manage that when he escaped," Byers said.

No, but he'd come close. But so had Byers. Considering the grenades, it wasn't much of a stretch to believe Byers was behind the other explosion, but Delaney had to ask.

"You put that bomb in my house?" she called out. "And left me that message?"

He didn't answer, but she could tell from the look in his eyes that it was a yes. And Delaney started to work out why he'd set up the attack that way. Byers had tried to make it look as if her father had caused the explosion, especially since Gil had been at her house earlier, and Byers could have done all of that so that Gil could take the blame.

And maybe that's what was going on here tonight.

"Byers wants my father to take the fall?" Delaney asked.

Cash made a sound of agreement. "Byers is almost certainly going to try to set this up as murder-suicide," he muttered. "After we've all been blown to bits, he'll make it look as though Gil got drunk and went off the deep end. I'm betting there's a letter or something that'll back that up."

Delaney was betting the same thing. While her father was drunk, Byers could have easily manipulated him into doing something like that.

"We have to get out of here," Cash repeated.

While he kept an eye on Ramone, Cash hurried to her father, hauling him to his feet. Gil was still wobbly, so Delaney threw down the pitchfork and took Gil's other side, shouldering him while they went to the back barn door.

"Wait a minute," Ramone interrupted. His voice was shaky and he swallowed hard. "What stops the SOB from just killing us when we go out there?"

"Nothing," Cash answered without hesitation. "But I'm betting this barn is about to blow."

Cash raised the board lock, easing the door open a fraction. "Help Delaney with Gil," he told Ramone. "And remember—if you double-cross us, you're a dead man."

"I'm not double-crossing you," Ramone insisted, hurrying to take Gil from Cash. "But I still don't think this is a good idea."

"It's not a good idea," Cash agreed, "but we don't have a lot of options. Unless we can get away from Byers and a grenade, either we can get shot or die in an explosion." Then Cash stopped, his gaze zooming to Ramone. "Can you call back the dogs? I want them to go to Byers, not my ranch hand who's lying unconscious on the ground by the shed."

Ramone's head whipped up, and he nodded. "They'll go to Byers since he's likely moving around."

Delaney prayed that was true. If not, Stoney could be mauled.

Cash was obviously having a debate with himself about that very thing, but he finally said, "Do it, Ramone. Call the dogs."

Moving fast, they went closer to the door, and Ramone gave a loud whistle. Within seconds, Delaney heard the dogs begin to bark.

"They'll attack Byers without any other command?" Cash asked him.

"Maybe. I got the Dobermans from somebody

who'd rescued them. I'm not sure what they'll do since they obviously still need a lot of training. That's why I've been keeping them in the pen."

Yes, they did need training, but maybe they could distract Byers enough for them to escape. Delaney only hoped Byers didn't shoot or hurt the dogs. She was terrified of them and thought they were dangerous without the training, but she didn't want the Dobermans to suffer or die, especially since it wasn't their fault they were trying to attack like this.

She listened for Byers to shout or make any sounds of distress, but the only thing Delaney heard was the frantic, agitated barking of the dogs. And her own pulse throbbing in her ears.

Cash opened the door wider, easing out while he whipped his gaze and his gun from one side to the other.

"Delaney, take the pitchfork with you," Cash instructed.

Ramone shifted, taking her father's weight so she could do that. But Delaney hoped it didn't come down to her having to use it. Still, she would. If it meant keeping them alive, she'd fight. Even if it meant fighting off Ramone. She didn't think the man was part of this attack, but just in case she was wrong about that, she'd keep an eye on him.

"Run for that big oak," Cash told them, and he tipped his head to the tree that was about twenty yards away. "Get down on the ground on the other side of it and cover your heads."

The oak was pretty much the nearest cover, but twenty yards gave Byers plenty of room to shoot them. Of course, from the sound of it, Byers was dealing with the dogs by ordering them to sit and stay.

Delaney paused long enough for her gaze to connect with Cash's. "What about you?" she asked.

"I won't be far behind you." He dropped a quick kiss on her mouth.

She wanted to make him swear that he wouldn't take any unnecessary risks, but at this point, everything was necessary.

"Call off these dogs!" Byers shouted, and he added some vile profanity to his demand. "Call them off or I'll shoot them."

Cash ignored him, and without looking back into the barn, he motioned for them to come out. When Ramone hesitated, Delaney used her free hand to help with her father, and she got them moving.

"Byers," her father muttered. "He's gonna try to kill you."

Yes, he would. Delaney had no doubts about that. But she kept moving, and the moment they were outside, they started running. Well, running as fast as they could considering her father was practically deadweight.

Each step seemed to take an eternity, and she focused on getting to the tree. And on watching Ramone. However, her thoughts—and fears—were with Cash. They had to make it out of this alive. They just had to.

The night air was heavy and humid. Smothering. And the smoke and stench from the burning porch made it hard to breathe. Still, Delaney dragged in as much air as she could and made a beeline for the tree. They were still a few yards away from it when all of her fears came true.

The explosion.

It came from behind her. The sound, heat and blast ripping through the night. It propelled them forward, tumbling them to the ground and knocking the pitchfork from Delaney's hand. She landed hard, her head smacking into a rock.

The dizziness came, the ground swirling around her, and Delaney couldn't move. Couldn't make her eyes focus. But everything inside her was screaming just one word.

Cash.

She had to get to Cash. She had to make sure he was okay.

Moaning, Delaney pressed her hands against the ground, trying to get up. She failed, but then someone was lifting her. She looked up into Cash's eyes.

He was alive.

But he was hurt. There was a gash on his head, and blood was sliding down the side of his face. However, that didn't stop him from running with her to the oak. He put her behind it and raced away. Delaney tried to take hold of him, to pull him back to safety, but she couldn't stop him.

She blinked hard, trying to will away the dizziness and clear her eyes, and she finally saw what Cash was doing. He was hauling her father to the tree. Cash had gone back to save him.

Ramone was limping along behind Cash and her father, but the man looked back over his shoulder. Delaney looked, too, and saw what was left of the barn. Which wasn't much. Byers had obviously used a grenade to blow it to bits.

"The dogs ran off," Ramone muttered, dropping down beside her father. "I hope they ran off."

So did she. But it was possible they'd also been hurt in the blast. Then again, if the dogs had still been close to Byers, he probably would have made sure he was out of range of the blast.

But where was Byers now?

Delaney didn't have to wait long for that answer. Byers stepped through the smoke, and in the moonlight, she could see the gun in his right hand. A grenade was in his left hand, and he had his fingers poised on the pin. If Byers pulled it, she was pretty sure the grenade would explode in a matter of seconds.

"If you shoot me," Byers warned them, "I'll have just enough time to toss it at you. You'll all die."

Delaney figured that was true, but with everything Byers had already done, she knew in her heart that he had no plans for them to walk away alive.

The black smoke swirled up around Byers, and the milky moonlight shone on his face. A face gone mad with the need for revenge. He looked like a demon who haunted people's nightmares.

"You were going to set up my father to take the fall for this," she said.

"Yeah." Byers's tone was flippant, but he cursed when he heard the sirens. His eyes narrowed. "He will take the fall. But Cash and you can save him by stepping out and letting me finish this."

Finish this by killing her.

If Delaney had thought for one second that Byers would be satisfied with just her death, she might have considered it, but there was no way he'd leave witnesses. Especially a cop like Cash. No. She figured the moment she stepped out, he'd fling the grenade, killing all of them.

"You're not going out there," Cash told her.

Her gaze met his again. The muscles in his jaw were tight. His mouth, in a grimace. But there was no madness here. What she saw was his fierce determination to keep her safe. However, this was out of his hands now since Byers was the one with the grenade.

"I have to do something before my deputies get closer," Cash added. "Get down and cover your heads again. I'm going to shoot Byers."

"You won't be down, and your head won't be covered," she reminded him.

Cash kissed her. "I'll be okay. Promise."

She was about to say that wasn't an assurance he could keep, but the growling sound stopped her.

Delaney whirled back to Byers to see one of the Dobermans leap through the smoke. The dog's powerful jaws locked onto Byers's arm.

Cursing, Byers twisted his body around. He lifted his gun, but he also pulled the pin.

Byers threw the grenade at them.

"Get down!" Cash yelled.

But he didn't do that. Cash remained standing, took aim.

And he fired.

Chapter Seventeen

The moment Cash fired the shot into Byers's chest, the man dropped to the ground. Cash didn't wait to see if his shot had killed Byers, because every second counted. He had to try to stop the blast from killing him.

"Cash!" Delaney called out.

He prayed that she hadn't started running toward him, but there was no time to tell her to stay put or get down.

Because the grenade went off.

The explosion sent a slam of heat and pressure right at him. A hard punch to every part of his body. Cash covered his head with his forearms and hands, but there wasn't much he could do for the rest of him. He had to lie there while the debris battered him as it flew from the blast.

Delaney called out his name again, and he cursed because she sounded closer than she had been just seconds earlier. He wanted her behind the tree, away from the fiery fragments coming at him like missiles.

While still keeping his head covered, Cash rolled to the side so he could see her. She wasn't behind the tree but rather to the side of it, and judging from the look of horror on her face, she thought he'd been hurt. Heck, maybe he had. Right now, it was hard to tell because his nerves were firing from the impact of the blast.

"Stay put," Cash told her. "Get down."

He did the same, but he had to turn back and make sure Byers wasn't coming after them again. However, it was hard to see anything in that direction because now there was a wall of smoke, dirt and heaven knew what else.

In the distance, Cash could hear the sirens. His deputies, no doubt, and maybe an ambulance and fire truck. They'd likely all be needed, but he didn't want any of the first responders hurt or killed. Something that could happen if Byers was still alive. The PI might take out any number of people while attempting to escape.

When the debris finally began to die down, the dogs started to bark and growl, and Cash heard Ramone belt out a loud whistle. "The truck," he ordered.

Cash thought the Dobermans obeyed because he heard them hurrying away. He couldn't tell how many of them were doing that, but maybe they'd all survived.

"You're hurt," Delaney said, and her voice was shaking.

"No, I'm fine," Cash answered, and to test that out, he forced himself to a sitting position. He took aim at the spot where he'd last seen Byers, but he still couldn't see the man.

Wincing from the bruises and cuts he'd gotten in the fall, Cash got to his feet and fired glances all around. Looking for any signs of another attack. Hard to tell that, though, when his backyard looked like the aftermath of a war zone.

Hell.

Smoke and debris filled the yard. The barn had collapsed, sending boards and beams as far as the eye could see. The ground was torn up, and there was a gaping hole where the last grenade had exploded. Cash suspected the back of his house would have similar damage. In fact, there might not be much left of his place.

One bright spot, other than them being alive, was that there'd been no livestock in the barn. Cash also didn't hear any sounds to indicate any of the dogs had been injured. He wanted to keep it that way. They'd all dodged a bullet, but that didn't mean more *bullets* weren't heading their way.

"Ramone, call 911 again," Cash instructed. "Tell the first responders to hold at the end of my driveway. I don't want them to approach until I'm sure the threat's been neutralized."

Cash wanted to go looking for that threat. For

Byers. He also needed to check on Stoney and his other ranch hands to see if they needed help. Or if they were even alive. But first he needed to make sure Delaney would stay put while he did that.

"Don't move yet," Cash reminded her.

With his gun ready, he went closer to where he'd shot Byers. There wasn't a clear path to reach the man, and Cash had to kick aside some debris and maneuver around the crater caused by the blast.

And then he finally saw Byers.

Cash's hand stayed on his weapon, but he was certain of one thing. Byers was dying. The man was sprawled out, his arms and legs at awkward angles, and the front of his shirt was covered with blood.

Byers moaned and then muttered some profanity. "You might have won, but Delaney still paid some. Not enough but some."

The man was wrong. Delaney had paid plenty. And why?

"Why did you do all of this?" Cash demanded. "Was this payback because of Webb's light sentence?"

"He got a slap on the wrist," Byers spat out. "I was going to let it go, but then Webb escaped. He was a free man, and that wouldn't have happened if he'd gotten a harder sentence to start with and gone to a prison where it wouldn't have been so easy for him to sneak out."

Cash could have pointed out that none of that was Delaney's fault, but he didn't bother to respond.

Unlike Byers who was obviously still seething with anger.

"After Webb was free, I wanted Delaney to pay and pay hard," Byers said, his tone full of venom. "I wanted everyone to think she'd lost it, that she was delusional, and then she would have been an easy target for Webb. Webb would have killed her, but he would have made her pay first."

Yes, Webb would have, and Cash was thankful both Webb and Byers had failed. Thankful, too, when Byers finally dragged in the last breath he'd ever take. Seconds later, the man's now lifeless eyes stared up at the night sky.

So there had been a casualty. A loss of life. Which wasn't much of a loss at all as far as Cash was concerned.

Cash didn't see any other grenades, but since it was possible that Byers had more on him, he didn't go any closer to the man. Once his deputies were on scene, he could have one of them get in a bomb squad. No use taking any unnecessary chances.

He turned when he heard the moan, and he looked past Byers and at Stoney. The ranch hand was sitting up and rubbing the back of his head.

"You okay?" Cash called out to him.

Stoney squinted against the smoke and gave a shaky nod. "Yeah. Somebody hit me with a stun gun."

Byers, no doubt, was responsible, and Cash hoped that meant Byers had done the same to the other ranch hands. Being stunned wasn't any fun, but it was far better than being killed. Maybe Byers had used the stun gun rather than shoot them because the shots, even those fired through a silencer, might have alerted someone. This way, Byers could sneak up on the hands and quickly disable them.

"Stay put for a couple more minutes," Cash told Stoney.

He didn't want Stoney stumbling around, tripping on debris. Or worse, stepping on a grenade. Plus, Stoney needed to be checked for injuries he might have gotten when he fell after being stunned.

Cash turned and headed back to the oak tree. He tried not to limp when he walked toward Delaney, because he knew it would alarm her even more than she already was, but he figured he failed big-time. His knee was throbbing like a bad tooth, but he could deal with the pain.

Yeah, he could deal.

Because Delaney was all right.

He didn't see any blood on her. No bruises or other visible injuries. That was something of a miracle, considering all the debris that had been flying around, and Cash would make sure she got a thorough examination since she'd hit her head when she fell.

"Byers is dead," he let her know right off.

"Dead," she repeated on a rise of breath. The sound she made was one of pure relief.

Cash made it to her as fast as he could and pulled

her into his arms. He needed this contact, needed to know that she was truly okay, but that need didn't blind him to taking precautions. That meant checking to make sure Gil and Ramone weren't about to launch their own attack. One look at the men, though, and Cash knew they had no intention of doing that.

Gil was sitting up, his back against the tree. There wasn't any fresh blood on his head, but he looked shell-shocked. Ditto for Ramone. His hands were shaking hard while he spoke with the 911 operator. If Ramone had had any plans to try to hurt them, he would have done it when Cash had been down in the yard.

"Go ahead and tell the responders they can come on the scene," Cash instructed Ramone. "They'll have to be careful, though, because there might be other grenades."

That put some fresh alarm in Ramone's eyes, but he relayed the information to the emergency dispatcher. Soon, they might be able to clear the grounds so they could get in an ambulance.

"You're really not hurt?" Delaney asked, drawing Cash's attention back to her.

"Just banged up a little. Nothing serious," he assured her.

That was the truth. If something had been broken, he was certain he would have felt it by now.

Cash leaned in and kissed her. Because he needed that, too, as much as he'd needed to hold her.

He'd nearly lost her tonight, and it might take him a couple of lifetimes to get over that she'd nearly been killed by a madman hell-bent on revenge.

He felt the dampness on her mouth and realized she'd been crying. On a sigh, Cash eased back, wiped away her tears and gave her another quick kiss. One that he hoped held the promise that he'd give her a much longer one once he was certain she was safe.

"Why'd you do it?" Gil muttered.

Cash pulled back enough from Delaney so he could look down at the man, but he kept his arm around her. He didn't want to let go of her until they'd both settled some more. Which, again, might take a lifetime or two.

"Do what?" Cash asked.

Gil pulled in a long breath. "Why'd you save me? You saved my life when you got me out of that barn."

Cash probably had kept him from dying, and he nearly gave Gil the line about it being his job, that it was just part of being the badge. And that was indeed true. But it'd been more than that.

"You're Delaney's father," Cash said simply. "She loves you."

Gil blinked hard, and the moonlight showed the tears pooling in his eyes. "I do love her." He groaned, shook his head. "And I nearly got her killed."

"I'm okay," Delaney insisted. She went to him and pulled him into her arms.

"No thanks to me. I didn't know what Byers was going to do. I swear it."

"I believe you." Delaney eased back to meet her father eye to eye. "Did Byers talk you into coming here tonight?"

Gil nodded. "He got me drunk, and I don't think straight when I'm drunk. Byers convinced me to come here."

"And do what?" Cash asked when Gil stopped.

"Demand that Delaney leave you." Gil looked up, stared at Cash. "He said as long as Delaney was with you, she could be killed. I wanted to believe him because I didn't want Delaney to be with you. But I can see I was wrong about that. You and Delaney belong together."

Well, that was a concession Cash hadn't thought he'd ever get from Gil, and he hoped that meant Delaney's father wouldn't give them grief about being together. Because Cash was going to do his best to talk Delaney into staying with him.

Delaney sighed. "I was the one who put Cash in danger."

"Not true." Cash hitched his thumb toward Byers. "Byers is the one who did this. He's the reason for the danger." He paused, kept his attention on Gil. "How'd Byers get to you? Did he find you after you left your house?"

Gil winced, probably regretting that he'd sneaked out on the bodyguard Delaney had hired for him.

"I'm not sure. I was walking from my house, and Byers was just there."

Byers had likely had Gil under surveillance, maybe hoping that he could use Gil to get to Delaney. And it'd worked. When Cash had let Gil into his house tonight, Byers had obviously put his sick plan into motion.

A plan to kill Delaney, Ramone, Gil and him.

Hell, maybe that plan had included anyone and everyone on the ranch if they got in his way. But the moment Cash had that thought, he heard Buck call out to him.

"Boss, you okay?" Buck asked.

He spotted the hand making his way from the bunkhouse, and Cash felt another wave of relief. "We're fine. How about you and the other hands?"

Buck staggered a little, but despite being unsteady, he still made it to Cash. "We all got stunned. We got some bumps and bruises in the fall, but we're okay. Where's Stoney?" Buck added.

"In the yard. He's all right, too, but I don't want him walking over here until the area's been checked for grenades."

Which would be soon, since Cash heard the fire truck and cruisers pull into his driveway.

"Wait here," Cash told Ramone, Gil and Buck. "I need to talk to my deputies."

"I'm going with you," Delaney insisted, taking hold of his hand.

Cash could have probably talked her into staying put, but the truth was, he didn't want to be away from her. "Stay right next to me," he instructed.

Delaney was already doing just that. She slipped her arm around him as they made their way around the remains of the barn and into the side yard. There was no damage here. No sign that Byers had even been on this part of the property.

When they made it to the front of the house, Cash spotted Jesse, who was already out of the cruiser. He'd brought three other deputies with him.

"What the hell happened?" Jesse asked, eyeing first the damage and then giving Cash and Delaney the once-over.

"Long story short, Byers tried to kill us," Cash explained.

Cash gave them a quick update, and they sprang into action, fanning out over the yard to check for any other explosives.

"Your house is burning," Delaney muttered. "I'm so sorry."

It was indeed on fire, and Cash had to accept that it might burn to the ground before the fire department could move in. It was a loss for sure, but at the moment, he couldn't feel any regret over it. He could always get another house. The same couldn't be said for the woman in his arms.

Because Delaney was the only woman he wanted.

"I'm in love with you," Cash told her. Yeah, the timing sucked, but he didn't want to go another minute without letting her know how he felt about her.

She looked up, and her eyes were surprisingly clear, considering they'd just gone through hell and back. "Good."

Delaney smiled. Kissed him. A long and deep kind of kiss that nearly made him forget that her "Good" was not the response he'd wanted to hear from her. Well, not the only response anyway.

"Good?" he managed to ask.

"Good," she verified, and distracted him with another kiss.

Cash decided to get in on that distraction. He hooked his arm around her, pulled her closer and added some heat to the kiss. Again, bad timing, but it felt *good*. It felt right.

The kiss went on way too long, and got way too hot, considering they had an audience what with the fire department and EMTs having arrived. Still, even when Cash finally tore his mouth from hers, he didn't let go of Delaney. He kept her in his arms.

"I'm in love with you, too," she muttered.

Now, *that* was the response he wanted. The response he needed. Just as he needed Delaney.

"Promise you'll tell me that often?" Cash prompted.

Delaney's smile widened, and he could almost taste that smile when she kissed him again. "Promise."

* * * * *

Look for more books in
USA TODAY *bestselling author Delores Fos-*
sen's series The Law in Lubbock County,
coming soon!

And don't miss the first book in the series,
Sheriff in the Saddle,
available now wherever
Harlequin Intrigue books are sold!

COMING NEXT MONTH FROM

ⓗ HARLEQUIN

INTRIGUE

#2091 MISSING WITNESS AT WHISKEY GULCH
The Outriders Series • by Elle James

Shattering loss taught former Delta Force operative Becker Jackson to play things safe. Still, he can't turn down Olivia Swann's desperate plea to find her abducted sister—nor resist their instant heat. But with two mob families targeting them, can they save an innocent witness—and their own lives—in time?

#2092 LOOKS THAT KILL
A Procedural Crime Story • by Amanda Stevens

Private investigator Natalie Bolt has secrets—and not just about the attempted murder she witnessed. But revealing her true identity to prosecutor Max Winter could cost her information she desperately needs. Max has no idea their investigation will lead to Natalie herself. Or that the criminals are still targeting the woman he's falling for...

#2093 LONE WOLF BOUNTY HUNTER
STEALTH: Shadow Team • by Danica Winters

Though he prefers working solo, bondsman Trent Lockwood teams up with STEALTH attorney Kendra Spade to hunt down a criminal determined to ruin both their families. The former cowboy and the take-charge New Yorker may share a common enemy, but the stakes are too high to let their attraction get in the way...

#2094 THE BIG ISLAND KILLER
Hawaii CI • by R. Barri Flowers

Detective Logan Ryder is running out of time to stop a serial killer from claiming a fourth woman on Hawaii's Big Island. Grief counselor Elena Kekona puts her life on the line to help when she discovers she resembles the victims. But Elena's secrets could result in a devastating endgame that both might not survive...

#2095 GUNSMOKE IN THE GRASSLAND
Kings of Coyote Creek • by Carla Cassidy

Deputy Jacob Black has his first assignment: solve the murder of Big John King. Ashley King is surprised to learn her childhood crush is working to find her father's killer. But when Ashley narrowly fends off a brutal attack, Jacob's new mission is to keep her safe—and find the killer at any cost.

#2096 COLD CASE SUSPECT
by Kayla Perrin

After fleeing Sheridan Falls to escape her past, Shayla Phillips is back in town to join forces with Tavis Saunders—whose cousin was a victim of a past crime. The former cop won't rest until he solves the case. But can they uncover the truth before more lives are lost?

HICNM0722

Don't miss the next book in

B.J. DANIELS

Buckhorn, Montana series

Order your copy today!

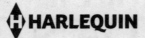

HARLEQUIN

Heartfelt or thrilling, passionate or uplifting—Harlequin is more than just happily-ever-after.

With twelve different series to choose from and new books available every month, you are sure to find stories that will move you, uplift you, inspire and delight you.

SIGN UP FOR THE HARLEQUIN NEWSLETTER

Be the first to hear about great new reads and exciting offers!

Harlequin.com/newsletters

Love Harlequin romance?

DISCOVER.

Be the first to find out about promotions, news and exclusive content!

Facebook.com/HarlequinBooks

Twitter.com/HarlequinBooks

Instagram.com/HarlequinBooks

Pinterest.com/HarlequinBooks

YouTube.com/HarlequinBooks

ReaderService.com

EXPLORE.

Sign up for the Harlequin e-newsletter and download a free book from any series at **TryHarlequin.com**

CONNECT.

Join our Harlequin community to share your thoughts and connect with other romance readers! **Facebook.com/groups/HarlequinConnection**

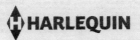